CW00376563

DON'T BREATHE

(A Taylor Sage FBI Suspense Thriller—Book 2)

Molly Black

Molly Black

Bestselling author Molly Black is author of the MAYA GRAY FBI suspense thriller series, comprising nine books (and counting); of the RYLIE WOLF FBI suspense thriller series, comprising six books (and counting); of the TAYLOR SAGE FBI suspense thriller series, comprising three books (and counting); and of the KATIE WINTER FBI suspense thriller series, comprising six books (and counting).

An avid reader and lifelong fan of the mystery and thriller genres, Molly loves to hear from you, so please feel free to visit www.mollyblackauthor.com to learn more and stay in touch.

ISBN: 978-1-0943-9459-6

BOOKS BY MOLLY BLACK

MAYA GRAY MYSTERY SERIES
GIRL ONE: MURDER (Book #1)
GIRL TWO: TAKEN (Book #2)
GIRL THREE: TRAPPED (Book #3)
GIRL FOUR: LURED (Book #4)
GIRL FIVE: BOUND (Book #5)
GIRL SIX: FORSAKEN (Book #6)
GIRL SEVEN: CRAVED (Book #7)
GIRL EIGHT: HUNTED (Book #8)
GIRL NINE: GONE (Book #9)

RYLIE WOLF FBI SUSPENSE THRILLER
FOUND YOU (Book #1)
CAUGHT YOU (Book #2)
SEE YOU (Book #3)
WANT YOU (Book #4)
TAKE YOU (Book #5)
DARE YOU (Book #6)

TAYLOR SAGE FBI SUSPENSE THRILLER
DON'T LOOK (Book #1)
DON'T BREATHE (Book #2)
DON'T RUN (Book #3)

KATIE WINTER FBI SUSPENSE THRILLER
SAVE ME (Book #1)
REACH ME (Book #2)
HIDE ME (Book #3)
BELIEVE ME (Book #4)
HELP ME (Book #5)
FORGET ME (Book #6)

CHAPTER ONE

Emily nibbled on her lip and bounced on her toes, hidden beneath a pair of flats she hoped weren't too casual for the occasion. A line-up of people spread before her, all waiting for admission to the United States Capitol building. Emily clutched her coffee in her shaking hands as the early morning sun caused beads of sweat to form beneath her bangs.

A few security guards waited at the entrance of the massive building. As sweaty and nervous as Emily was, she glanced up and marvelled at it. She was really here. The Capitol dome reached proudly into the afternoon sky, and the white building shone like ivory in the sun.

All her life she'd been waiting for this day. Someday, she wanted to join Congress herself—but starting as an aid to the esteemed Senator Corbin Ryan was a start. The line continued, and Emily breathed in and out, practicing the techniques her therapist had taught her to keep her anxiety in check.

I already have the job. I don't need to be so nervous!

Two security guards greeted her: one behind a desk, the other standing by a metal detector.

"Your ID and reason for visit?"

"I'm Senator Ryan's new aid? He should be expecting me. Oh, here, I have ID—" Emily went to reach into her purse for her ID card, just as the burning coffee cup squeezed a bit too hard in her hand—and slipped right out.

Boiling hot liquid seared Emily's chest as the coffee dumped all over her. She screamed and jumped back. Not only did it burn like heck—but her crisp white blouse was now a horrible shade of brown.

Emily had always been a klutz. But this was truly the worst moment of her life.

"Miss, are you okay?" the security guard asked, his face bewildered.

Right—Emily was still in front of people. She was being watched. Totally embarrassed, she stammered, "I, um—I'll be right back!" and bolted out of the Capitol building.

Her mind raced. This was a disaster, but maybe she could still fix it. Sometimes she kept extra clothes in her car. Yes—she probably had a sweater in there. It wouldn't look the best, but anything would be better than coming into the senator's office covered in java.

She hurried toward the parking garage, trotting down the steps until she was underground, surrounded by concrete and cars. It was cooler down here, and the smell of gasoline filled her nose. The sound of her shoes clacking resounded through the underground parking lot. She picked up her pace. If she didn't hurry, she would not only show up looking like total crap—she'd show up late.

But as she was passing by an entrance to another stairwell, a shadow caught her eye in her periphery. Emily did a double-take before she looked over.

A woman sitting on the ground, her back slouched up against the wall.

She had platinum blonde hair covering her face, and was dressed in business-casual—it looked like a pencil skirt and a blazer with a blouse underneath. She was also completely motionless.

Emily paused. Was this lady drunk or something? For a moment, Emily felt slightly better about her situation. Sure, she was a mess at the Capitol—but this person was way messier.

Don't be mean, she scolded herself. *Maybe she needs help. I should go see if she's okay.*

Emily glanced at her watch. 7:49 a.m. She had to be in Senator Ryan's office in eleven minutes. She didn't have time to check on some passed out, drunk lady. It so wasn't her problem.

But as she went to pass, she realized she couldn't just leave the poor thing, either. She imagined herself in that situation: how awful it would have been if someone had just left her like that. She'd had more than her fair share of drunk all-nighters, after all, so she got it.

Emily sighed and trotted up to the woman, whose blonde hair shielded her face.

"Excuse me, miss. Are you okay?"

No response.

Emily approached until she was right next to the woman. Emily glanced over her shoulder, an uneasy feeling crawling through her.

"Hello? Miss? You okay down there? Have one too many mimosas?"

Still silence.

Damn it, I don't have time for this!

Emily leaned right in to grab the woman, but that was when she saw it.

A stab wound pierced right through the center of the woman's chest, a pool of blood staining her shirt.

Emily stumbled back and barely had time to contain her horror before her screams echoed, again and again, through the garage.

CHAPTER TWO

Special Agent Taylor Sage flipped the pancakes simmering in the pan, the smell of warm maple in her kitchen. The morning sun poured through the back window as her husband, Ben, poked the bacon around next to her. Taylor slid a couple of pancakes onto the plate on the counter, then went to add another patch to the pan.

"Honey, don't forget to add more butter first," Ben said, not looking at her.

Taylor hesitated, hand still holding the measuring cup full of batter. "Oh. Right…" She scooped some butter out of the tub and lobbed it into the pan, creating *pops* and *sizzles* in the air. She added the batter, zoning out as it began to caramelize on the bottom side. Heat radiated off the pan, so warm and mesmerizing, when—

POP.

Taylor flinched as the bacon next to her popped loudly. Ben shot her a frown.

"You okay, honey?"

"Fine, fine…"

But it wasn't fine. Taylor ran her hand over her abdomen, where a phantom pain grew. Was this where she was at now—triggered into a flashback just by cooking breakfast?

Two weeks had passed since she'd started back at work again. And it'd been even longer since she was discharged from the hospital. Summer was drawing to an end, and the shadows were growing longer. Soon, kids would be going back to school.

Kids. Taylor didn't even want to think about them.

After the tarot reader's ominous warning—that someone was going to leave her soon—Taylor hadn't mustered up the strength to tell Ben the truth about what she found out at the hospital. That because of an old wound, she would never be able to give birth. His dream—their dream—of starting their own family had been ripped away permanently, and there was no going back.

It would devastate him. And while she had every intention of telling him, after the visit to Belasco's, it became harder each day. Taylor had once believed that Ben would stand by her no matter what. But now, all because of some stupid card, she just wasn't sure.

But holding this in was like keeping a malignant growth on her heart, slowing eating at her soul every day. It would probably kill her soon. Every night, she went to bed next to Ben, knowing she was lying to him. Sometimes they had sex, sometimes they didn't. When they did—she felt the guiltiest of all. Because afterward, he would say things like, *"I'm so glad we're trying now,"* and *"I can't wait to start our family."*

Every *"I love you"* with him was tainted now. And Taylor had to sit there with the fact that she knew damn well they were never starting a family. Not in the traditional way, the way Ben wanted, and had wanted the entire time she'd known him.

Fuck. I have to tell him. But how?

"Taylor? Taylor!"

Ben's voice snapped her from her daze. A burning smell wafted up from the pancake in front of her, and smoke rose into the air. Taylor yelped and moved the pan off the burner.

"Jesus, hon!" Ben shouted, fanning the air with a towel. "Are you trying to burn the place down? What's wrong with you?"

Taylor clammed up. This was all too much. How much longer could she go on with this charade? Hugging herself, she stormed away from the stove. She heard Ben clicking off the burners before he followed her into the living room.

"Taylor. What the hell is going on?"

She couldn't face him. Her eyes burned. Was this really how it was going to go down? On a normal morning, making breakfast?

Ben, calmer now, moved in front of her. She didn't look up at him as he grabbed her arms. "Taylor, what's going on? I've been trying to work with you, but… you've been acting strange. Ever since you left the hospital, you've just been different."

Taylor dared to look up into Ben's brown eyes. The eyes she loved so much. He scanned her face before he smoothed his thumb over her cheek. But Taylor pulled away, and hurt darted over his face.

"What is this?" he asked, getting emotional himself.

"Ben, I…," she trailed off. "I just don't know what to say."

"Taylor, if something happened… you can tell me. What is it? Is it your partner?" He paused, his voice thick with emotion. "Are you having an affair?"

"What? No!" She was appalled he could even think that—Taylor was extremely dedicated to Ben. She'd never *cheat.*

"Then what the hell is going on with you?" His eyes were bloodshot and desperate. Taylor's stomach did a million flips.

It's time. You have to tell him.

She tried to think it in her father's voice, as if it would give her strength. But her father would never be as weak as she'd been over these past weeks. She knew her father would have told her to tell Ben the truth immediately, and she should have done that. Now things were going to be way worse, because not only could she not have kids, but she'd lied about it for weeks.

Taking a breath, Taylor tapped into her subconscious mind. Into the parts of herself that were closed off emotionally, the parts of herself that were unafraid. The parts she always unlocked at work. It felt weird to apply to her relationship, but at this point, maybe there was no other way. In order to tell the truth, she needed to stop being Ben Chambers's wife and start being the strong agent she knew she could be.

So, she relaxed her jaw. She stifled her tears. And in a calm voice, she said, "Ben, we need to talk."

Tensely, they sat on their living room couch, a full cushion away from each other. Ben leaned forward and clasped his hands together. "Oh God, it's an affair, isn't it?" His voice cracked.

Taylor shook her head. "No. It's not that." She drew a shaky breath and looked down at her hands, at her wedding ring. This was the moment. Then, she forced herself to meet his eyes. "Ben, when I was in my mid-twenties… I was shot."

Ben flinched. "Shot? Where? You never told me."

"No, I didn't. And I'm so sorry, but…" Looking away, she lifted her shirt, which revealed the scar on her abdomen.

"Your appendicitis scar," Ben said. "You said it was surgery when you were sixteen."

"I'm so sorry. I lied."

Ben's scowl deepened. Taylor's stomach flipped again.

"So, what, it's a gunshot scar instead?" Ben asked. "Why did you lie about it? And what does this have to do with *anything?"*

It has to do with everything. Another deep breath. Time for the truth.

"The shooting was trauma I didn't want to relive, Ben," Taylor said. "The truth is, I was ashamed of the circumstances that led to it because I had been, well… I'd been reckless. Like I was with Jeremiah

Swanson. But the consequences were even more severe. I actually didn't realize how bad it was until the hospital."

"What do you mean?" Ben looked at her with an innocent but concerned curiosity.

"Ben…" Taylor sighed. *No more lying. No more games.* "I swear, I didn't know this until I went to the hospital. But the doctor told me that when I was shot, it did permanent damage."

Confusion flitted across Ben's face before Taylor was sure she saw awareness. Like he was finally starting to understand where she was going with this.

Swallowing a knot of dread, Taylor said: "Ben, the doctor told me I can't have kids."

Ben blinked. Once, twice, then his eyes fell to the floor. His face twisted, like he had a migraine. "No—what? That can't be right. We've been trying. We've…"

"Ben." Taylor blinked out tears. The pain in her heart was so severe, she felt like she couldn't catch any air. "I'm sorry. It's true."

Abruptly, like a rocket, Ben stood up. Taylor closed her eyes, taking comfort in the darkness. She couldn't bear to watch. But she could hear him—Ben pacing around the living room, his heavy footsteps thumping against the hardwood of their new home. The home they'd moved to with plans to start their own family.

"Taylor, tell me you're not serious," he said.

She didn't reply. Didn't look at him.

"Taylor!" he yelled. His booming voice caused her to pop her eyes open and face him. He'd never yelled at her, not like this, and she'd never seen more desperation on his face. Slowly, she stood.

"I'm so sorry I lied," was all she could say.

Ben clutched his head and paced back and forth. "Taylor, this isn't a small lie. This is our future. This is *my* future. All I've ever wanted is—"

"A family. I know. It's why I couldn't tell you. It was too hard, Ben."

"I can't believe you would hide this from me. It's been weeks—we've been sleeping together, and that whole time, I thought we were trying for a *fucking* baby!"

Taylor flinched. In all of their years of marriage, Ben had only sworn at her a few times, and even then, it was never directed at her like this. Heartbreak was written all over his face, and she blinked out more tears. What else could she do? She didn't ask to be shot—but she had created this situation by lying to him for so long. She should have told him the moment she found out. As her husband, it was his right to know.

"I know this was cruel of me," she choked out, "and I really am sorry. But—" She walked up to him and grabbed his hands, hoping she could fix this. Ben just looked down at her, betrayed. "But we can still have a family, Ben. There are other ways. We could adopt, we could—"

"Are you serious right now?" He ripped his hands away and took a step back. "I don't want to talk about this, Taylor. I can't just accept this. We need to see more specialists. There has to be a way. Do you think I want to raise someone else's kid?"

His words were biting. And Taylor could hardly believe them. Was the prospect of adopting so disgusting to him? She had married a kind and generous man. One she knew wanted a family. But she never imagined Ben would speak in such disdain, when he knew how many children there were out in the world who needed homes.

"You don't have to be so harsh," she said.

"Harsh? Really, Taylor?" Ben threw his arms up again. "You have got to be fucking kidding me. You lied to me for weeks, and—" He sighed, pinching the bridge of his nose. "You know what? Never mind. This is pointless. I want you to book an appointment with a fertility specialist so we can get to the bottom of this."

Taylor's throat tightened. There was no point in going to a specialist—somehow, in her heart, she knew the doctor had been right. Maybe her subconscious had always known, and that was why she'd hesitated on having kids for so long. If they went to a specialist, it would only prolong this torture and give Ben false hopes.

"Ben, I'm sorry," Taylor said. "Seeing a specialist won't change anything."

"Like hell it won't." He stormed into the kitchen and grabbed his phone. Taylor watched, her heart pounding as he angrily typed something in. "Here. There's a fertility specialist downtown. We can go see her, and maybe she can fix this."

"You mean fix *me.*"

Ben met her eyes. And for a moment, empathy bled through his anger, but he said nothing.

"I get it," Taylor said. "You think I'm broken now."

"Taylor," he said carefully, *"you're* not broken. You're my wife, who I want kids and a life with. And just because one doctor said you can't, that doesn't mean it's the truth."

She didn't want the answer to this question, but they were already in the depths of the fight now, so she asked: "Is that what we won't have if I can't have kids? We won't have a life together?"

Ben was stunned. The naïve part of her wanted him to break down and say how sorry he was for being so harsh, to tell her that he'd be with her no matter what—that they could adopt, or do literally anything else to make this work. Taylor had always wanted kids, but Ben was already in her life—she had chosen him. And he chose her.

But now, he couldn't muster up a reply. He opened his mouth to speak when Taylor's phone buzzed in her pocket. Ben turned away, saying nothing, so she checked it.

It was Calvin Scott. Her partner. She wasn't sure why, but relief flowed through her. Like Calvin could somehow save her from this awful moment.

Ben was already in the kitchen, clutching his head. He clearly wasn't going to answer her question, so she picked up the phone.

"This is Taylor Sage."

"Special Agent Sage, it's me," Calvin said.

"Hi, Scott. I know it's you."

"You all right? You sound sick."

She kept her posture straight, wiping a tear from her eye. "No, I'm fine. What's going on?"

"I need you to meet me at the US Capitol building." He paused; Taylor's heart raced. "We have a new case."

CHAPTER THREE

Caution tape barred off an entire portion of the US Capitol's lawn as Taylor approached. More than a few officers and security guards were stationed throughout the property, and the show had garnered a slew of spectators on the street. Taylor briskly approached a security team near the entrance. It was mid-morning, and the late-August sun was hot beneath her long-sleeved black shirt.

As Taylor drew closer to the building, she made out a familiar form: Calvin Scott in sunglasses, hands in the pockets of his slacks as he talked to an officer. Taylor walked up, and Calvin spotted her. He nodded at the other officer before he jogged down to meet her.

"Sage, I'm glad you're here."

"What's going on?" Taylor asked. She could not fathom why on earth she had been brought to the US Capitol building, of all places. Its magnificent dome reached into the mid-morning sky, radiating a power that had spanned throughout history. Taylor had only ever been here for a tour when she was a child, with her father, mother, and sister. She buried the memory, unnerved that Angie had once been here with her.

Calvin placed his hand on her arm and led her onto the lawn so they could talk in private. He removed his sunglasses, revealing the imprint on his nose and his blue eyes. Sweat pooled on his hairline.

"As I'm sure you can tell by all of this," Calvin said, gesturing to the caution tape and officers around the building, "there's been a murder."

"Here?" Taylor gasped.

"That's right. Over there, more specifically." He gestured to the entrance of the underground parking lot, which was completely taped off. Calvin went on, "Because it happened on federal property, they decided to call us in right away rather than go through D.C.'s police force. Although the other cops are down there documenting the scene."

"How was the body found?" Taylor asked.

"I don't have all the details yet—I haven't been down. Was waiting on you. Come on, we have a witness inside—I wanna talk to her ASAP so the poor thing can go home, then we'll do the rest of the dirty work."

Nodding, Taylor followed Calvin. They went through the entrance of the Capitol and encountered some security guards. Taylor and Calvin showed their badges, gaining access to the building. Taylor could feel the history in its regal walls, and they walked down a long corridor, their shoes clacking against the shining tiles. Two officers were stationed outside of one of the rooms; Taylor and Calvin showed their badges once again, gaining access to it.

Inside, a young woman sat alone at a desk, jittering. There was a fireplace behind her and American flags hanging. Her mousy brown hair was tied back, but strands flew up in every direction. She bit on her nail and didn't seem to notice Taylor and Calvin enter.

Taylor cleared her throat, and the girl nearly jumped out of her skin.

"I apologize," Taylor said. "We didn't mean to startle you."

"O-oh, it's okay." She placed a hand over her heart. She was wearing a blouse with a massive coffee stain on it. "It's been, well, a hectic day…" The girl laughed awkwardly.

Taylor exchanged a look with Calvin, before she said, "We're with the FBI. I'm Special Agent Taylor Sage, and this is my partner, Agent Calvin Scott."

She nodded. "I'm Emily. Um—Emily Fitzpatrick."

"Do you mind if we take a seat and talk about what you saw today?" Taylor asked.

"Oh, um, yeah, of course," the girl rambled on anxiously. Calvin was right—this poor thing looked like she'd need therapy for the rest of her life. Taylor decided they would make this quick.

The two agents sat on the opposite side of Emily. Calvin awkwardly cleared his throat, adjusting his shirt, while Taylor clasped her hands on the table. Emily was pale with freckles, and her lips looked borderline blue—she was clearly still in shock, so Taylor made a mental note to go easy on her.

"I know this is traumatic for you," Taylor said, "so please don't rush yourself. But can you tell us what happened this morning?"

"Ah, well…" She flicked her hand across her arm, as if scratching a phantom itch. "I was so scared I was going to be late for my first day—and I'm such a klutz, and I spilled coffee all over my blouse, as you can see…" She tried to laugh, but Taylor got the sense it was a defense mechanism to cope with what she really saw. She understood that well. But a look of horror then appeared in Emily's brown eyes.

"What happened next, Emily?" Taylor pressed.

"Um..." She hugged herself, sinking deeper into the chair. "It was..."

"There's no pressure," Calvin cut in. "Take your time. Tell us when you're ready."

Emily sucked in a breath. A few moments passed. Sunlight leaked through the window on the wall, and Taylor anticipated her response. She didn't want to rush or pressure the witness—but her anxiety was rising. *Come on, tell us. We need to know.*

"Okay," Emily blurted. "Okay. I was going to my car in the underground parking lot to see if I had any extra clothes to cover this mess, and then I saw... her. She was lying against the wall. I thought she was drunk..."

A chill ran up Taylor's spine, remembering the last case she and Calvin had worked on. One of the witnesses had said they thought one of the victims was a drunk teenager. Memories from the case threatened Taylor's mind—memories of both her and Calvin almost losing their lives. But she stuffed them down.

"So you couldn't tell she was deceased right away?" Taylor asked.

"No, not at all, I went up to see if she was okay and..." Emily shuddered. "She was bleeding out of her chest!"

A shooting or a stabbing? Taylor wondered.

"Did you recognize her at all?" Taylor asked. "Was there anyone else around?"

"No, and no," Emily said. "I just screamed for help... the rest is sort of fuzzy." Emily leaned her elbows on the table and ran her hands through her hair, stressed. "Oh, man, I really need this job. If Senator Ryan doesn't want me anymore—"

"That won't be an issue," Calvin said. "We'll make sure you keep your job. This wasn't your fault by any means. And hey, after this, I think you deserve some time off. We'll make sure you get paid for that too."

Emily nodded, vaguely smiling. But then something else seemed to hit her, and she said, "Oh, but if there's someone killing women around here, then—"

"Security will be increased tenfold," Taylor assured her. "And we'll find whoever did this. I promise."

"Thanks, agents..."

Taylor stood up, and Calvin followed suit. She focused on Emily. "Thank you, Emily, for your time and your statement. Please keep yourself available in case we need to speak again—but until then, an officer will be happy to escort you home."

With that, they left the room, Emily still jittering at the table. But Taylor had gotten all she needed from her—it was time to see the body.

***

Taylor moved past the caution tape and went down the stairs that led into the underground parking lot. The concrete roof blocked out most of the sun, making it as dark as night. Taylor had always found underground parking lots unnerving—she'd come across more than a few cases that involved a shooting or stabbing in one of them, so this felt eerily familiar. Although she wasn't sure how much worse it could get than the last big case they worked.

Calvin was close behind her. They didn't talk as they followed the caution tape and stream of police officers until the crime scene came into sight. That familiar feeling of unease returned to Taylor's bones, the one she always got when she was about to see a dead body.

A tall, lean man with silvery hair stood, sunglasses pushed onto his forehead, wearing a cop uniform, and watched the scene. He looked like he was in charge. Officers were taking photos. Taylor's eyes followed the flashes, where she finally saw her: the woman leaned up against the concrete wall, slumped over. A spot of red clear through her blouse. Platinum blonde hair fell over her face.

"Shit," Taylor muttered.

The silver-haired man noticed the agents and immediately approached. Taylor and Calvin took out their badges, flashing them quick. The man nodded.

"Good, I'm glad you're here," he said.

"Special Agent Taylor Sage," Taylor said. "This is my partner, Agent Calvin Scott."

"I'm Chief Mike Sanders. I'm not usually first on site at my age, but this one..." He glanced at the body. "It happened right on government property. This seemed like it needed a special eye. That's why we called you feds in right away."

"Do we have an ID on the victim?" Taylor asked.

Sanders shook his head. "No ID on her yet. But something about this woman is familiar... I can't quite place it. Nothing we've seen so far has given us any clue about who killed her."

Taylor nodded. "I better take a closer look."

The officers taking photos cleared away as Taylor and Calvin stepped in. Calvin hung back slightly while Taylor took a closer look. Her eyes skated over the woman's torso. A single slice was ripped into the bloody fabric. Definite stab wound, and it looked like only one. On top of that, there wasn't a drop of blood on the concrete floor, so there was no way the murder had happened here.

Whoever did this killed her somewhere else and dropped her here.

But as Taylor looked farther up the woman, a sense of shock hit her—she recognized her. She had seen her face on TV. She flipped through her mental channels, trying to place her, until she remembered.

"I know her," Taylor said out loud. "Not personally—but Scott... this is Margot Withers."

Calvin's brows pinched. "Wait, that sounds familiar. Is she...?"

"The woman who accused that senator of sexual misconduct," Taylor finished for him.

"Shit," Calvin said. "I remember hearing about that."

Taylor got down on one knee and leaned forward. It would be easier to see if she brushed the victim's hair away, but she didn't want to disturb the scene. Plus, she was certain in her conviction anyway. This was, one hundred percent, Margot Withers.

About a month ago, Taylor had seen her on the news. She remembered it clearly—it was when she was at home with Ben after the incident with Jeremiah Swanson, and they were on the couch, watching TV in the living room. The news reporter claimed that an unknown source had come forward with the news that Margot Withers, a young secretary, was accusing Senator Frank Petit of sexual misconduct. She claimed he had groped her while she was working for him, and that the incident caused her deep emotional distress. But it wasn't Margot herself who was coming out with this—some other whistle-blower came out, forcing Margot to go public.

It ended up being a political firestorm, and Margot was caught in the middle. She eventually went on the record claiming it was meant to be dealt with privately, but someone had leaked it to the press. Democratic senators began using her as fire on Republicans, while the Republicans were accusing Margot of making the whole thing up. But Taylor hadn't heard anything on the case in at least a week. It had fallen from her mind entirely.

Now, Margot was dead.

"This is her, Scott," Taylor said.

"Jesus," Calvin said. "Think we have a political conspiracy on our hands?"

"It's a hell of a coincidence." She stood up, brushing her sweaty palms on her pants. "The whole scandal seemed to calm down in the public eye, but that doesn't mean it wasn't still going on behind the scenes."

And Taylor didn't want to waste time on hearsay. To find out more about Margot, there was one place Taylor wanted to look first—one place not tainted by political conspiracies or biases.

She met Calvin's curious stare. "Let's go talk to the family."

CHAPTER FOUR

When Taylor had seen Margot Withers on the news barely three weeks ago, she never expected she'd be arriving at the house she grew up in. Taylor and Calvin had left their cars parked on the road and were now walking up to the house. It was a nice place—colonial-style front, very classic American. The flag stood proudly on their lawn. Taylor could see why Margot ended up in politics; she clearly came from a patriotic home.

A bad feeling churned inside Taylor as she and Calvin stepped onto the front porch. She hadn't had to confront a family about the death of a loved one since their last case, and that hadn't been easy, but it was something she'd been doing almost her entire career. But a new anxiety racked at her. Maybe it was because of the fight with Ben—she tried to shove it into the darkest corners of her mind, but even if she wasn't directly thinking of Ben, she could still feel the aftereffects of the fight in her body. It was like she'd been injected with a dose of pure anxiety, bubbling through her veins.

Not only that, but as far as she knew, the family hadn't been informed yet. This would make Taylor and Calvin the messengers. Which could look a lot different than talking to someone who was already grieving.

Either way, Taylor knocked on the front door and waited. Margot's parents were retired—Taylor had learned that while looking up their information. A pickup truck was in the driveway, so she figured someone must be home. After a few moments, a tall man—quite muscular for his age—opened the door. He peered down at Taylor and Calvin beneath graying, bushy eyebrows.

"Can I help you folks?" he asked.

"Um, hello," Taylor said, immediately embarrassed she had stuttered. That wasn't like her. But even though she knew it was her job, she didn't want to look this father in the eye and tell him his child had been killed.

Taylor choked up, so Calvin swept in and said, "Are you Tom Withers?"

“That’s me.” Tom leaned one arm against the doorframe, a distrusting look on his face. “Can I help you?”

Calvin glanced at Taylor. Her heart was pounding wildly in her chest, and her throat felt like it was as tight as a kite string. *God, what is wrong with me?*

Normally, she’d be doing most of the talking, but Calvin clearly picked up that something was wrong, so he said, “We’re with the FBI. I’m Agent Calvin Scott and this is my partner, Special Agent Taylor Sage. Do you mind if we come in?”

Tom suddenly straightened his posture. “Federal agents, welcome. Of course you can come in.”

Everything about Tom’s persona felt patriotic and military-esque. This wouldn’t make the news any easier to break. Taylor stepped inside the house after Calvin and found herself surrounded by war memorabilia on the walls: medals, World War II photos, and a photo of Tom himself in what appeared to be Afghanistan.

But there were pictures of Margot too. As a baby, as a child, as a teenage girl. That platinum blonde was all natural. It was so easy for the press to exploit her when they wanted to—using her beauty as a way to paint her as an “unfavorable woman.” But she was just an ordinary girl, who had parents who loved her.

Images of her body flashed in her mind. It all made Taylor sick.

The three faced each other in the foyer. Tom put his hands in the pockets of his jeans. “Everything okay, officers? I don’t suppose this had anything to do with the harassment my daughter has been receiving?”

Taylor glanced at Calvin, momentarily comforted that she wasn’t alone in this awful situation. She cleared her throat and said, “Is your wife home?”

The fact that something was wrong was clearly starting to register on Tom’s face. His brows pinched, and he said, “Marianne is home, yeah. Should I get her?”

“Please,” Taylor choked out.

Tom nodded, then gestured to a doorway that led to a living room. “You two go sit down.”

As ordered, Taylor and Calvin went into the living room and awkwardly sat on the floral couch. Taylor flattened her slacks and held her knees together. She felt Calvin looking at her in her peripheral vison. Taylor didn’t want to explain anything, but he leaned toward her to whisper, “Sage, are you okay? You seem way off today.”

Although Taylor's anxiety still clawed at her, she forced a nod. "I'm sorry. I'm just—my head's not in it. This is never easy."

"Do you want me to tell them?"

"No. Let me."

Maybe it was her stubbornness, but Taylor felt like she owed it to these people—and to Margot—to find the strength to tell them herself. She didn't want to be a coward and let this sudden anxiety win. *She* wasn't the victim here—Margot was. So were her parents. Whatever petty drama Taylor had going on in her own personal life would have to wait.

After a few moments, Tom returned with a spindly woman with a bright smile, who could only be Marianne Withers. Dirt splattered her gardening apron, and she had deep crow's feet and laugh lines on her tanned face, evidence of a life spent happy. Once more, Taylor's chest sank.

"Hello, agents," Marianne said. "So sorry for the mess—if we'd known we were having company, I'd have cleaned up a bit more."

Taylor couldn't bring herself to return Marianne's smile. All of this was breaking her heart and was dragging on far too long. "We don't want to take up too much of your time," Taylor said. "Please have a seat."

The smile melted off Marianne's face. She and Tom exchanged a look before they took the loveseat.

"Is everything okay?" Marianne asked, eyes bouncing between Taylor and Calvin.

"I was thinking it was about all those threats Margot was getting," Tom mumbled gruffly as he crossed his arms over his wide chest.

Taylor took a breath. The longer she drew this out, the more painful it would be. "Mr. and Mrs. Withers, I'm… very sorry to have to tell you this."

The color immediately drained from Tom's face. As an obvious war veteran, he clearly knew what those words meant. But he remained stoic as Marianne blinked at Taylor, waiting for her to continue.

Taylor's throat constricted again, but she managed to say, "Margot was found dead this morning. She was murdered."

Tom breathed in sharply, his blue eyes blearing over in a flash. But he kept his posture as straight as an arrow. Marianne, on the other hand, had a look of disbelief on her face.

"I'm sorry, that's a mistake," she said. "I talked to Margot yesterday. It must be someone else, I—"

Marianne stopped herself. Taylor's heart dropped into the pit of her stomach, but she held eye contact as best as she could. "I'm sorry, Mrs. Withers. You will be called in to ID her, but… I saw her myself. I know Margot from, well, the case, and the news…"

"No, that can't be!" Marianne abruptly stood up. "It has to be someone else; it has to be! Margot was fine. She *is* fine. I promise you; you're mistaken."

Tom stood up and grabbed Marianne's shoulder, steadying her. She was still looking at Taylor, devastated, and Taylor wished she could disappear into the floorboards. But Tom's grip on his wife grew firmer, and he forced her to meet his eyes.

"Marianne, go upstairs. Let me deal with this."

"They're wrong," she said, shaking her head. "It's not her. It's not our—"

"I'll deal with it," Tom said. "Go upstairs. Please."

"But where is Margot?" Marianne ripped her arm away, anger contorting her face as she refocused on Taylor and Calvin. "I knew getting deep into those political games would get her hurt, I knew it!"

"Marianne, go upstairs," Tom said again. This time, he gently urged her away. Marianne looked like she wanted to slap him. But with one last look at Taylor, she rushed into the hallway. Seconds later, her footsteps were heard on the stairs, and her sobs echoed through the house. A door slammed shut.

That was bad. Really bad. Out of all the reactions to death a person could have, Taylor always found denial to be the most difficult to cope with. To have to not only tell somebody their loved one was dead, but to *convince* them, made an already impossible task that much more difficult.

But as bad as Taylor felt, she had to get this ball rolling. Now that Tom was alone with her and Calvin, Taylor cleared her throat and faced him. He tried to keep his posture strong, his dignity intact, although not even his miliary training could hide the pain he felt from this.

"I'm so sorry for your loss, sir," Calvin said.

"Thank you, son." Tom sniffled once, his blue eyes bleary, his jaw trembling.

"We'll do our best to keep this brief," Taylor said. "Can you tell us more about the threats Margot was receiving?"

"It was all those damn, slimy senators… both sides of the political spectrum," Tom uttered. "They were all just using her to push their own agendas. And that rat senator who groped my daughter—he's the worst of them all."

Taylor could easily agree that Frank Petit was a shitbag. But on the drive over here, she'd called Winchester and asked for some quick recon on Petit, only to learn he was on vacation in Cuba and had been for two weeks to "get away from it all." But that didn't mean he wasn't somehow involved in Margot's death; it just meant he didn't do it himself.

"Do you know who specifically was sending the threats?" Taylor asked. "Were they from Senator Petit?"

"I don't know," Tom replied. "Margot only showed me a few. They were pretty unhinged. I doubt they were from Petit himself, but they had to be from one of his cronies. One of his cronies had to have done this too."

Another thought occurred to Taylor: if Frank Petit had anything to do with the murder, it would be extremely bold of him to let it happen on government property. Life-altering levels of stupid, actually. It wasn't totally impossible—she'd seen people get caught for extremely stupid crimes before, many times throughout her career. But Taylor needed to know more about those letters to help determine who was sending them.

"Do you have the letters?" she asked.

"No, not here. We don't have any copies of them. But Margot said she printed them off as proof. She might have them back at her apartment. She left home for her internship, didn't want to make the drive…" Tom's fist balled, and his jaw clenched tighter. "I knew I never should've let her leave home."

Tom was trembling, on the verge of breaking at any moment, and Taylor took that as her cue to leave. The poor man needed to grieve, and Margot's apartment was the best place for them to start.

Taylor stood up, and Calvin followed. She bowed slightly at Tom, who couldn't bear to look at them. Wiping her sweaty palms on her pants, Taylor said, "Thank you, Mr. Withers. We'll check the apartment. And we're sorry again for your loss."

"Thank you," he croaked out.

Taylor went to leave. But she had one more thing to say to him first.

"We'll find who did this. I promise."

Tom's eyes met hers again. This time, a fury burned in them past the tears. "I believe you," he said. "I'm counting on you."

Taylor nodded. It was a promise she had every intention of keeping. Whoever did this was going to pay.

CHAPTER FIVE

Taylor slid a woman's suit, dry cleaned and covered in plastic, aside in the closet. Margot Withers clearly had both style and money; the items in her closet ranged from business chic to business casual, like the things Taylor wore herself, only ten times nicer. As Taylor and Calvin had been working through the girl's apartment, Taylor had started picturing more and more about what her life had been like. And it didn't make this any easier.

When she'd seen Margot on TV only weeks ago, Taylor remembered thinking that the girl looked elegant and classy, like she was wise far beyond her years. At only twenty-one, Margot somehow managed to hold the air of a dignified thirtysomething. She'd had a bright political career in front of her—her aspirations went beyond being an assistant to a man.

Taylor remembered hearing her on TV, saying, *"My goal is to become a senator myself, and never mistreat those who are still working their way up the ladder."*

She would have been an inspiration to girls everywhere. But she died before she even got the chance.

No, she didn't just die, Taylor reminded herself. *She had her life stolen from her. Big difference.*

It was all the more motivation for Taylor to keep going.

Moving on from her closet, Taylor approached Margot's desk. Her bed was neatly made, and her whole room looked like something out of an IKEA catalogue. Outside in the living room, she could hear Calvin rifling around in the bookshelf for a clue. Taylor had told him it'd be more appropriate if she searched the girl's room alone. She was trying, as best as she could, to respect Margot's memory.

Taylor approached the desk, where a planner was splayed out next to a gold pen. There was a pencil holder and a framed photo of Margot hugging a large Samoyed dog. Oddly, it reminded Taylor of a high school student—which also reminded her how young Margot truly was. She was fresh out of college and looking forward to her twenty-second birthday. Taylor thought of herself at that age, and her stomach curled. She couldn't imagine not living the past decade of her life—so many important things had happened. Falling in love, becoming a police officer, and then fulfilling her lifelong dream of being a federal agent. All of this was making her feel very humbled. No matter what she had going on at home with Ben—Taylor was grateful every day for the life she had.

But another unsettling thought clawed its way to the forefront of her mind. Taylor's sister, Angie, didn't get the chance to live her life either. She had disappeared even younger than Margot was. Who would Angie have become if she hadn't gone missing? She was presumed dead. But Taylor still didn't want to believe that. They never found the body, after all.

She stifled down the thought. She had work to do on a case that had a much bigger likelihood of being solved. Carefully, she opened one of the drawers on the white-painted desk. The first drawer contained several notebooks that seemed filled to the brim; Taylor briefly skimmed them, only to see they were mostly old planners and journals, dated a few years back.

Taylor moved onto the next drawer, not wanting to dig up anything too personal that wasn't relevant to Margot's death. And as far as she was concerned, the trail would begin a few weeks ago, when Margot's accusation leaked to the press. She was probably living a completely normal life until Senator Frank Petit decided to be a piece of shit.

Tugging at the second drawer, Taylor discovered it wouldn't budge. She tugged at it again, and the desk rattled. Damn it—it was locked. She scanned the surface of the desk for a clue, but there was no sign of a key anywhere, only pencils, pens, erasers, and other odd knickknacks.

Closing her eyes, Taylor tried to picture what it was like to be Margot. She seemed like a smart girl. Resourceful. If she wanted to hide something…

Maybe plain sight was the answer.

When Taylor opened her eyes, the framed photo of Margot and the dog was the first thing she saw. It was a longshot, but she flipped open the back of the frame.

Front and center was a tiny silver key.

Taylor's heart leapt. Finally, progress. Jamming the key into the lock, Taylor opened the second drawer. Inside was a stack of letters.

A knock startled her. Taylor whipped around to see Calvin leaning against the doorframe to Margot's room, hands in his pockets. His casual posture showed her he hadn't found anything of value. "Any luck?" he asked.

Taylor nodded and flashed him the stack of letters in her hand. Calvin took the invitation to come in and check it out, peering over Taylor's shoulder as she splayed them on the desk.

"Damn, good find, Sage," he said.

"Thanks," she mumbled. Her hands shook with anticipation. These letters were their biggest clue, and she didn't want to waste another second not reading them.

One by one, both she and Calvin began to open and read the letters. The first one Taylor opened had a professional-looking layout, with a neat serif font. It read:

Dear Ms. Withers,

I hope you understand the gravity of what you are doing. Senator Frank Petit is a good and honest man. You are needlessly throwing away your own career and damaging Senator Petit on a baseless claim that could simply never be proven.

Revoke your claims at once, and this can all go away.

The sender had no name.

But the next letter Taylor opened was different. It wasn't on a neat page—rather, a piece of lined paper. And the scrawl on it looked nothing like the neat writing from the last letter. It read:

You're making a big mistake. BIG BIG BIG. Stop now OR ELSE.

It wasn't signed by anyone. But this had to be a different person from the other letter.

Beside her, Calvin flipped through his stack. Taylor caught a glimpse of them to see they were mostly the lined paper ones as well, with that same garbled scrawl.

"Some of these are pretty nasty," he said.

"Agreed…" Taylor trailed off, opening another letter. More scrawl. More horrible words. "No outright death threats, but enough to look into, that's for sure. We need to find out who these are from."

"There's a lot here, Sage." Calvin began to sort the letters into a neat stack, then checked his watch. "It's getting late—maybe we should call it. Let the techs sort out the senders tonight, and we can reconvene tomorrow. What do you think?"

He was right; they were even farther than D.C. now and had a long drive ahead of them back to Quantico, and even farther for Taylor to get home to Pelican Beach. Still, Taylor had that nagging feeling inside her—the one that implored her to just keep working.

But that mentality was exactly what had made things so strained with Ben on the Jeremiah Swanson case. And after the bomb Taylor had dropped on him this morning… didn't she owe it to her husband to at least come home?

A sigh, and Taylor nodded. For now, they would put this to rest—but first thing tomorrow, she would be back on the case.

***

Taylor walked into her house and locked the door behind her, only to find the lights were all off. Hours on the road had her eyes feeling sore, but it was still too early for Ben to go to sleep; he usually stayed up until ten, sometimes eleven. But the house was quiet and still, and his car was in the driveway.

I guess we aren't talking tonight, Taylor considered. At least she could sleep next to him; his warmth beside her would at least remind her that she was safe. But when Taylor got upstairs and checked their bedroom, she found their bed still made, and no sign of Ben in it.

Taylor's heart sank, her pulse thrumming. Thoughts raced though her mind. Did he leave? But his car was still there. Did he take a cab somewhere else? Go out drinking with some people? Panicking, Taylor hurried down the hall to check the guest room next.

And there he was, sound asleep, curled on his side with his back facing her.

Even if he was asleep, the cold gesture caused Taylor's stomach to flip. She wanted to cry, to wake him up and make everything right—but maybe there was no coming back from this one. At least not tonight. She had to give her husband some space, so she wandered back to the bedroom and changed into her pajamas, beginning her nighttime ritual. As she brushed her teeth, images of the murder scene flashed in her mind; Taylor was certain she'd be tossing and turning all night, unable to sleep.

Still, she found herself yawning as she turned off the light and crawled into bed. And when she hit the pillow, she was surprised by how heavy her body became. Soon, she drifted into a dead sleep. Dreaming of nothing at all, until—

A voice called to her, deep within her subconscious. *"Taylor! Taylor!"*

She knew that voice, but she hadn't heard it in so long. It was a distant memory, overshadowed by the sands of time, by the years that had ticked on…

"Taylor!"

Who are you? Where are you?

The voice became clearer, and the image with it. Like an apparition, Angie appeared before Taylor. They were on a street of some kind, surrounded by trees and fog. Like the spot where Angie had gone missing.

Taylor couldn't believe what she was seeing. It was her sister, in the flesh. So real she could reach out and touch her. Tears stung her eyes. "Angie?" she croaked out. She was the same person she had always been: black hair and gray eyes, just like Taylor, but with a softer face. More gentle, more kind. However, right now, she looked older. Like an Angie in her late thirties. An Angie that Taylor had never seen before.

But in a flash, her sister was gone.

Panic took hold of her. She didn't think—she just ran, searching everywhere, like she had in the forest all those years ago during the search party for Angie. Somehow, she knew exactly where to run. She'd been there before. The clearing in the forest where they'd found the shred of Angie's clothing. It was the only trace of her the police had ever found, and in her youth, Taylor had visited the spot many times.

But this time, when she got there, it wasn't a shred of Angie's clothing.

Angie's mangled body lay ahead of her, bloodied and torn to shreds. This time, she looked just like her teenage self; the Angie that Taylor remembered.

"No!" Taylor screamed. She ran up to her and landed next to her body, her knees skidding in the mud. "No, no, Angie! I just got you back, I just—"

A loud ringing cut Taylor off and reverberated through her mind.

Taylor's eyes popped open to her bedroom ceiling in the dark, her clothes and sheets drenched in sweat. Her heart pounded in her ears, sending ripples of pain to her skull. Her chest heaved as she regained her consciousness.

A nightmare. That was all it was.

But it was the most vivid nightmare she'd ever had.

Angie—she had been so real. The emotions from the dream still lingered, just as real as if it had truly happened. In that sense, it was more like a flashback—although Taylor never saw Angie's body. No one did.

Snapping out of it, she turned her attention to her nightstand, where her phone was ringing and vibrating. The clock read six a.m.—there was only ever one person who called her at this hour.

Sure enough, it was Calvin Scott.

"Scott, what's going on?" she answered.

"Sage, I need you to get dressed quickly," Calvin said, his voice rushed. "We have a lead to run down."

CHAPTER SIX

In the passenger seat of Calvin Scott's car, Taylor flipped through more letters as Calvin drove them toward an apartment building in a run-down D.C. neighborhood. The tech team had managed to track down the sender—they had come from a man named Joshua Smith, a licensed gun-owner with a history of assault and battery.

As Taylor read through more of the letters, each became more deranged and unhinged. Taylor's stomach curled at the one she'd stopped on:

Margot Withers,

Stop. STOP NOW. If you don't, THERE WILL BE CONSEQUENCES.

Her skin crawled. *Consequences like what, Josh?*

Murder?

And the next one:

You have no idea how important this senator is, Ms. Withers. You're making a terrible mistake. You're just a pawn in their game. Don't you see that?

She wondered what kind of game he'd convinced himself they were playing.

On the drive up, Calvin had briefed Taylor on everything the techs had found in the letters and all the dirt on Josh Smith. Apparently, he believed Margot was some sort of "deep state pawn" who was tasked to take down Senator Frank Petit, who was actually a very important, high-up member of some sort of secret government organization. *Great,* Taylor thought, *a conspiracy theorist.* She'd dealt with more than a couple of those throughout her career, and they were always the most difficult to reason with. So detached from reality that there was little to say to get through to them. And it wasn't uncommon for someone like that to be a murderer—not at all. Anything for the cause, right?

They pulled up to the building, a three-story walk-up with dumpsters overflowing in the parking lot. Calvin's car bumped over potholes as they found a spot in the visitors' parking area. A hunched-over woman with straw-like hair walking her dog glanced over at them as they exited the car, giving them the stink eye. Taylor had a bad feeling about this one—especially the whole "licensed gun-owner" thing, as the guns he was apparently "allowed" to use were shotguns and rifles. For hunting, his file said. But Taylor's gut feeling said otherwise.

And after all her past experiences, she was learning to trust that feeling. She touched her belt beneath her jacket—her handgun was there. Good.

As they entered the building, which smelled of mildew and cat urine, they found their way to the third floor. Calvin pulled out a piece of paper from his pocket—their search warrant—as they moved down the dingy hallway with flickering lights.

"It's apartment 310," he said. "We might be met with some resistance, so be ready."

"Agreed," Taylor said.

Once at 310, Calvin knocked. No answer. He knocked again—still no answer.

"Hello, Mr. Smith? Are you home?" Taylor called in, knocking on the door as well. "This is the FBI—we have a warrant to search your apartment. If you don't open up, we'll be forced to come in."

Silence. Taylor and Calvin exchanged a look.

"Maybe he really isn't home," Taylor said.

"Well," Calvin said, tucking the warrant away, "we have the right to go in anyway. So let's do this. Watch my back, okay?"

"What are you—"

Before Taylor could protest, Calvin slammed into the door. It was cheap and old, and after another strong boot, the lock busted, and the door flew open. Taylor looked at Calvin, shocked he'd been so bold.

"Hey, I can't be bothered waiting around," he said.

Taylor shrugged. They had a warrant, after all, so their means of entering was hardly her concern. What was important was getting Josh's dirt.

They entered the dark apartment. It was small and dingy, and Taylor flicked on a light, revealing a confederate flag on the wall and a coffee table cluttered with hunting magazines and ashtrays. Lovely. This guy was clearly a pack rat, as boxes bursting with papers piled halfway up the wall, and there were cases upon cases of empty beer bottles. Not to mention the *smell,* like a wet, beer-soaked rag. It all made Taylor want to throw up.

"Well, shit," Calvin said, looking around at the chaos. "Where do we even begin?"

Taylor sighed. There was a lot of junk here—sorting through it would take weeks. "Let's just dive in and hope for the best."

Calvin began with the boxes while Taylor took a different approach. Josh probably kept more personal belongings in his bedroom, so she crept down the hall to find it. Every part of this apartment was as messy as the last; the bathroom was littered with old laundry, and as Taylor found her way to the bedroom, her nose was assaulted by a foul smell. She tried not to gag as she entered the man's bedroom and turned on the light. His bed was unmade, and more dirty laundry scattered the carpet, which had several stains on it. There were posters of naked women on the walls mixed with gun propaganda and another confederate flag.

But there was one photo on the wall—a large, IKEA-style black and white picture of D.C.'s skyline—that stood out. *Bizarre,* Taylor thought. This photo stood far apart from the others. Maybe it was a gift from his mother or something. It was definitely out of place.

Moving on, she went into the closet, where she found another pile of clothes and a stack of boxes filled with random papers. This man was clearly a degenerate and not well—but a bunch of filth didn't say he was a killer. It just made the letters to Margot even creepier.

Just as Taylor was thinking this was going nowhere, she turned back to the black and white photo. It just didn't fit with anything else in the room, and it took up nearly the entire wall. Maybe it was a longshot, but something in her told her to check behind it.

Taylor went up to the photo and removed it from the wall. It was shockingly light, made of wood and canvas, and she set it off to the side.

But what she saw on the wall beneath the photo made her stomach bottom out.

Pictures upon pictures of Margot Withers were pasted in a full-blown board on the wall. Pictures of Margot from afar, walking down the street, having coffee in a café, shopping downtown. Pictures of Margot getting in her car—arriving at the Capitol building.

Taylor's mind raced. Holy shit. This was their guy.

"Scott, get in here!" she called out.

No response.

"Scott!" Taylor repeated, eyes still glued to the wall. But no answer came. "Damn it, Scott," she mumbled to herself, storming back into the living room, frustrated she had to repeat herself. Why wasn't he listening?

But when she got to the living room, Taylor's heart stopped.

Calvin was standing with his hands up as he faced down the barrel of a shotgun.

A man—who Taylor could only assume was Josh Smith—pointed his gun straight at Calvin. He was thin, wearing a vest with patches on it, with long, greasy brown hair and leathery skin, despite being only thirty-one years old. He didn't react to Taylor's presence in the room, just said, "Make a wrong move and I'll shoot."

Taylor stayed still, her heart battering her ribcage. The danger of the situation dawned on her, making her sweat. *Not again. It can't end like this.*

"Sir," Taylor carefully said, and Josh's eyes flicked to her, "we're with the FBI. We have a warrant to search your apartment—please lower your weapon."

"Like hell you're from the FBI. I know exactly what you two are—and why you're here!" Rage contorted his face as he stormed up to Calvin, still pointing the gun. Calvin eyed the barrel, but somehow kept himself together.

Taylor considered her options. She could go for her gun and shoot, but that would be a risk to Calvin's life. Josh could shoot that thing at the slightest wrong move, and then Calvin's organs would be wall paint.

Her second option was to try to talk her way out of this. He didn't seem like a reasonable man—far from it—but she'd dealt with worse. She just needed to watch her tone, and be very, very careful with her words.

Heart pounding, Taylor cautiously said, "You're Josh Smith, right? Please, we don't mean you any harm. We're with the police. We just want to talk. Talk about the things you know. We're on your side, Josh. We're against them too."

She hoped the talk of "them"—whatever nameless enemy he had in mind—would help calm him down. But it didn't work.

"Talk?" Josh's voice raised. "Are you kiddin' me!? You come in here and rifle through my private property, and you wanna talk? Tell me why you're really here!"

"Okay, okay," Taylor said. If her other plan didn't work, then maybe this would: "We're investigating the death of Margot Withers."

"She's *dead?"* A strange look Taylor couldn't place covered Josh's face. It might have even been a moment of despair and confusion but was quickly replaced by more anger. "Well damn straight she is, damn government spy!"

Taylor scowled. This didn't seem like the reaction of somebody who already knew Margot was dead. But still, all signals were pointing to Josh. And Josh's gun was still pointed at Calvin.

"We understand you were sending Margot letters," Taylor said, taking a wary step closer to Josh, who seemed to be loosening up. He lowered the gun from Calvin's chest to his torso—which was still not safe enough to make a move, but better.

"I didn't kill her, if that's what you're thinking," Josh said, "but damn straight I would've liked to. Damn. Who got her?"

"Please lower your gun so we can talk," Taylor said, still cautiously approaching. If she could just get within reach…

"Damn bitch was a narc of the highest degree," Josh rambled. "Frank Petit is an important part of all of this. and that bitch was trying to take him down. Who hired her? Do you know?"

The moment Josh lowered his weapon more, Calvin dove out of range. Taylor sprung to life—she had to act fast. She tackled Josh to the ground before he could process that Calvin had moved, before he could fire that shotgun. Josh tried to shoot, but Taylor pried his finger away from the trigger.

"Bitch!" Josh exclaimed. He put up more of a fight, and Taylor had to usher up every bit of her strength to keep him from firing that weapon.

Thankfully, Calvin swept in. He kicked Josh hard in the leg, causing him to yelp in pain as his grip loosened on the weapon. Taylor ripped it from his hands, then tossed the gun to Calvin, who caught it with ease. In a flash, the shotgun was now pointed right at Josh. With his back flat on the ground, he shot his hands up as fear widened his eyes.

"Okay, okay, shit!" he exclaimed. "Don't shoot! I'll talk, I'll talk!"

Taylor forcefully flipped Josh onto his stomach and twisted his arms, causing him to retch in pain. She pulled his bony wrists together and slapped cuffs on him.

"Joshua Smith, you're under arrest in relation to the murder of Margot Withers."

As she began reading him his rights, a sense of justice surged through her. Even if this guy wasn't Margot's killer—she had a damn good feeling behind bars was where he belonged. But first, he was coming with them to Quantico so they could find out every bit of information he had.

CHAPTER SEVEN

Taylor eyed Josh Smith through the double-sided glass as he sat in the interrogation room. He was handcuffed to the chair but rattling around like a manic. Taylor and Calvin were just waiting for him to waste his energy before they went in.

"Piece of shit," Calvin muttered.

Taylor looked up at him. His brows were furrowed as he watched through the glass, still pale from earlier. Calvin had managed to keep it together, but he and Taylor had barely talked since they booked Josh Smith. Taylor was getting to know Calvin pretty well by now, and she could tell staring death in the face had shaken him up. She didn't blame him for that.

"You okay?" Taylor asked. "It's not every day you face down the barrel of a shotgun like that."

Calvin glanced at her, forcing a small smile. "I'm okay, Sage. Thanks. Just pissed I didn't see it coming."

Hindsight is always twenty-twenty, she reminded herself. How many cases had she worked where her life had needlessly been in danger? If only she could have predicted the future—"seen" things like Belasco seemed to—then she never would've gone into that warehouse where she got shot all those years ago. If that hadn't happened... Taylor's life would be looking a hell of a lot different now.

Sighing, Taylor turned back to Josh, who seemed to have wasted the last of his energy thrashing in the chair. Defeated, he sagged with slumped shoulders like the sad sack he was. After seeing the disturbing content in his apartment, the last thing Taylor wanted was to treat this guy like a human being. But it was her job to get the truth, and sometimes, that took a bit of calculation.

"Should we do this?" Taylor asked, and Calvin tensely nodded.

They entered the room together, and Josh jolted awake as they did. Taylor, taking the lead, slapped a folder down on the table and sat across from Josh, while Calvin sat next to her. Josh tried to lunge out of his chair again. Neither agent flinched—he wouldn't be getting out of those restraints any time soon.

"Joshua Devin Smith," Taylor said, flipping open his file. "It seems you have quite the history. Breaking and entering, attempted arson, stalking…" Taylor's gaze flitted to Josh. His beady brown eyes glared back at her. "And now murder."

"I didn't kill no one!" Josh exclaimed, rattling his cuffs behind the chair. His angry face reminded Taylor of a rabid dog, foaming at the mouth.

"It's okay, Josh," Calvin cut in, playing the good cop. "If you just tell us exactly what happened to Ms. Withers, we promise you'll be treated fairly and with respect. Respect is something you value, isn't it?"

Josh said nothing, just glared.

"But if you don't, and try to resist," Taylor said, "we won't be able to help you. I should remind you that we found the little shrine to Ms. Withers in your bedroom. I have to say, with her being found dead, this isn't a good look for you."

Josh's eyes flared along with his nostrils.

"So it's really best if you just tell us the truth now," Calvin said. "Just tell us what happened. Help us help you, and this can all go away."

"I'm telling you the damn truth," Josh spat. "I didn't kill that bitch Margot. Did I follow her around? Okay, fine, I did that. And yeah, the pictures are mine, so what? So maybe I was tracking her, but I didn't fuckin' kill her!"

Josh's broken vocabulary and consistent cursing made him even more disgusting to Taylor, and she hated the idea that somebody like this could have stolen a bright young woman's life away from her. Taylor didn't want to waste too much time on the good cop/bad cop play—she wanted this guy to confess so they could get this over with.

"Josh," Taylor said, "we have evidence, hard evidence. And now your confession that you were stalking the victim. You keep weapons in your home. How long do you think—"

"Go ahead and search my whole place!" Josh shouted. "You won't find nothing 'cause I didn't fuckin' kill her. And you know what? I'm pissed off I didn't. I'm pissed 'cause I was *gonna.*"

Taylor and Calvin exchanged a look. This was going in an odd direction, and Taylor wasn't sure what to make of it. But something was telling her that Josh wasn't lying. Why would he admit to the stalking and wanting to murder her if he didn't actually do it?

"You were *going to* kill her?" Taylor pressed.

"Yes, damn it!" Josh heaved out a massive sigh, slumped in the chair. "I was gonna. Okay? But I didn't. Somebody else did. They beat me to it, the piece of shit."

Taylor didn't know what to think. Josh seemed genuinely envious that "somebody else" got to kill Margot. But if not him—then who?

"And who would you suggest that might be?" Calvin asked before Taylor could.

Josh sighed and glanced around the room, like he was checking to see if there were more cameras than the one blatantly pointed down at him. "All right, look," he muttered. "I dunno if I should be sayin' this. This could get me in big trouble, you got it? So be careful who you tell, agents… be careful who you trust, 'cause *anyone* could be listening."

Oh, boy, Taylor thought. But she figured it was better to let the man speak; even an incoherent ramble could prove useful, so she stayed quiet.

"Look, I wasn't the only one who had an eye on Margot Withers," Josh said.

Taylor's ears perked. Most of what Josh had been saying seemed like utter bullshit to keep him out of trouble. But this made her want to listen.

"Who else?" Taylor asked.

"There was this guy. I'd see him a lot. You know, when I was keepin' an eye on Withers, learning her schedule. I used to see this other guy—don't think he ever saw me and Withers herself didn't seem to notice him tailing her neither."

"Can you describe this suspect?" Taylor asked.

"I dunno, man. Tall, sort of. Definitely a guy. He always wore a black baseball cap, sunglasses, and a black sweater, even if it was hot as hell out there. Skinny-looking guy."

Taylor squinted, searching Josh's gruff face for any sign of a lie. But she couldn't read him, anyway—he was too unhinged, eyes bugging out and flitting all over the room. As compelling as the idea of another stalker was, he had to be full of shit. Guys like Josh were all about "freedom" and maintaining their rights while also oppressing others. He made her sick to her stomach. Why should she give him the benefit of the doubt?

Besides, they'd checked his alibi before the interrogation, and it was flimsy at best; the landlord said he was home but couldn't really *confirm* if he was or not. They also weren't short on the motive for murder, so all they needed now was a murder weapon—the knife that killed Margot. Either way, Joshua Smith was guilty enough to detain.

Taylor stood, nodding at Calvin, giving him the signal that they were done here. Josh rattled around in the chair again.

"Hey, where the hell are you goin'? I'm tellin' you, I didn't kill that bitch! Let me out of here!"

But Taylor and Calvin were already breezing toward the door. Taylor glared at Josh once over her shoulder before she left the interrogation room.

On the other side, Chief Steven Winchester stood with his arms crossed over his wide chest—Taylor could only assume he'd been watching and listening to the whole thing. Winchester looked like he'd gotten a haircut—his military-style cut was shorter and trimmer than usual, but he still had that handlebar mustache.

"Good work, agents," the chief said. "I heard everything. We have a solid case here."

Taylor definitely agreed—it was a solid case. At the same time, she had that niggling feeling in her gut, similar to when they arrested Mark Johansson when it was really Jeremiah Swanson who they were after. All signs were pointing toward Josh being guilty. So why didn't Taylor feel like she'd solved the case?

"Do you think there's any merit at all to what he said?" Taylor asked. "About the other stalker?"

"Not a chance," Winchester said. "We have forensics searching for the murder weapon now. It's best we close this thing fast—the last thing we need are a bunch of senators and aids thinking there's a killer on the loose. This is clearly our guy."

Taylor looked at Calvin for his input, but he just shrugged. "The guy pointed a shotgun in my face. I'm not about to defend him."

"So it's settled then," Winchester said. "Great work, you two. Hey, I know it's still early, but why don't you take the rest of the day off? We can handle things here."

Normally, a day off would sound nice—but a sense of panic immediately struck Taylor.

If she wasn't at work—that meant she had to go home and face Ben.

"Are you sure, sir?" Taylor asked. "Because—"

"Of course I'm sure!" Winchester bellowed a laugh, slapping both Taylor and Calvin on the shoulders. "You two deserve a break. Go on, enjoy your day off."

"Thanks, Chief," Calvin said. "I really could use it."

While Taylor wasn't as eager, she followed Calvin into the hallway of the Quantico HQ. His pace was brisk, and Taylor increased her stride to keep up with him. She did not want to go home yet. And since she was technically still new here, she hadn't exactly made friends—Calvin Scott was the closest thing she had. Some quality time outside of work with her partner might be good for her soul. Plus, she was hungry.

"Hey, Scott," she said, winging it, "did you maybe want to grab lunch or something?"

Given their experience together so far, Taylor assumed he would say yes. But Calvin hesitated, before saying, "Sorry, Sage, I'd love to, but I can't."

"Really? What are you doing?" She didn't mean to pry, but they just found out they'd had the day off, so how could he already have plans?

"Just… some personal stuff I gotta deal with at home," he said. They stopped at the end of the hallway and faced each other. Calvin smiled. "Another time though, okay?"

Taylor nodded. She didn't want to show that she felt the cold sting of rejection; it wasn't exactly easy for her to "hang out" with people. Taylor didn't do friends; she just had Ben, her family, and whatever coworker made it into her work sphere.

She just nodded. "Of course. See you tomorrow."

Calvin smiled once before he left though the doors, leaving Taylor in the hall, contemplating their interaction. His behavior was a bit odd—the Calvin Scott she knew would never turn down a lunch, especially since on the Jeremiah Swanson case, he'd been so interested in making sure Taylor was eating. But he probably did have personal matters to attend to. Taylor decided not to take it personally.

She also wasn't going home to Ben, not yet. There was a disaster waiting there in the form of her husband, and maybe it was cowardly of her—but facing that beast was one thing she didn't want to deal with. It was ironic, she thought, how she had built a life around taking down dangerous murderers but could not muster up the courage to face one of the kindest, gentlest men she'd ever known.

With a heavy heart, Taylor left the Quantico headquarters, grateful for the warm sun on her skin. She found her car in the parking lot and got in, alone. Looked like she was driving around solo.

CHAPTER EIGHT

Pelican Beach's boardwalk stretched before Taylor, basking in the afternoon sun. The waves glistened as they rolled onto shore, and the salty smell of the sea surrounded her. Taylor wasn't sure how she even got here; it was like she'd been moving on autopilot. After she left Quantico, she simply drove where her heart took her. Now, her shoes clacked against the wooden boardwalk beneath her, reminding her of the time when she and Ben got ice cream before they met Madam Belasco for the first time.

Nice memories flowed through her mind. Taylor may not have realized it, but in hindsight, she had been so much more optimistic back then. Optimistic about this new job, the new town, their new life. Images of Ben's easygoing smile made her stomach sink.

There were so many things she wished she'd done differently.

Told the truth, for one. Two, if she'd checked on her fertility sooner, then maybe they could've done something to save her before the damage was so severe. That was probably a pipe dream too, as Taylor had been shot directly in the abdomen. But still, as she wandered around, lost in her own mind, she allowed herself to dream a little about another life where everything went right. She continued along the boardwalk, listening to the waves and the sounds of people laughing and talking as she passed.

Darker memories crept in. The pain of the bullet striking her abdomen all those years ago. The hospital, only a few weeks ago, and the look on the doctor's face when she broke the news. Taylor knew she'd lost the life inside her all those years ago… but she never would have guessed that one event would still affect her, so many years later. Permanently. A thought occurred to her: Taylor had spent so much time worrying about how Ben was going to feel about her being unable to bear children, that she had barely spent any time thinking about how *she* truly felt about it.

Running her hand along her stomach, she relished in the feeling of the sun on her face. To think that she'd never carry a child there made her feel numb. Maybe she was supposed to cry, to ask whatever god why they chose this, but in reality, Taylor just felt robbed and powerless. There was nothing she could do to reverse the damage, so now she had to live with it, to find a way around it.

If she did decide to have a family, adoption was probably the best option. But in all honesty, right now, Taylor had a hard time picturing her or Ben being stable enough to even consider starting a family for real.

She wasn't even sure how she felt about Ben right now at all. She'd be lying to herself if she said he'd been a nice, caring husband through all of this. In fact, he hadn't even acknowledged Taylor's own trauma, too focused on himself. His selfishness—frankly—pissed her off. But he was still her husband, who had treated her so right for so many years. Taylor couldn't just let go of the good memories—even if things were horrible right now.

God, what have I gotten myself into?

Veering back toward downtown, Taylor was still moving on autopilot. Past benches and trees erected on the sidewalk, past groups of people shopping and milling about. Her mind wandered. There was something else she hadn't been able to shake, something she didn't want to face. And that was the dream she'd had about Angie the other night.

It had felt so real. Like Angie had truly been there, right in front of her. And the strangest part was, the way Taylor had seen her, it was like she was a grown-up version of Angie—like what Angie might look like now if she were still alive. Maybe that was just Taylor's brain tricking her, remembering things wrong and making things up. The dead version of her sister, however, had looked exactly like how Taylor remembered Angie as a teenager. She had pictured that scene many times, even if she never actually saw it with her own eyes. Nobody did.

Pulling herself from her reverie, Taylor lifted her head. The sights around her were familiar—the dress shop across the street, the bench with the garbage can next to it. She looked up.

Above her was the sign for Madam Belasco's shop.

Taylor paused. She hadn't been in since she got her last reading, which had rightfully freaked her out. But what were the chances of her absentmindedly ending up here again? Maybe it was a sign. Belasco had helped her before—maybe she could again.

Taking a deep breath, Taylor entered the shop, surrounded by the familiar scent of incense burning. The door chimed. It was dark, and when Belasco didn't immediately come out, Taylor had a moment to second guess the decision. After all, the last time she'd been here, she'd left incredibly anxious.

But before Taylor could make up her mind, the curtain opened, and Miriam Belasco stepped out. As always, she appeared elegant and poised, dressed head to toe in flowing purple clothing with gold accents and jewelry. Large gold hoops dangled from her ears. She looked at Taylor with wise eyes, like she'd been expecting her.

"Mrs. Sage," Belasco said in her smooth, sultry voice. "It's lovely to see you again."

"Uh, yeah, hi." Taylor ran her hang along the strap of her purse, realizing she was still in her work clothes. "I was just hoping to get a reading, but if you're busy—"

"It's been a slow day," Belasco said, holding open the curtain. "Why don't you come on back?"

With a lump in her throat, Taylor followed Belasco into the back of the shop. She'd grown too familiar with its statues of pyramid-like figures and all-seeing eyes. Belasco already had her tarot cards set up on the table, and like every time they had met, they each took their respective chairs facing each other.

Belasco began shuffling the cards. She peered at Taylor beneath long eyelashes, purple makeup rimming her eyes. "How have you been? It's been weeks since our last meeting. I've been thinking of you."

Taylor knew what she was really asking—if the prediction came true. As far as Taylor knew, Ben hadn't left her and was still at home, angry, but waiting. He hadn't immediately filed for divorce. Taylor had to believe in her heart that he wouldn't do that, either. She had to believe that he would try for her, at the very least, and not just walk out the door.

"I've been all right, thanks," Taylor said, clamming up. She wasn't here for a therapy session. And one of the things she liked about Belasco was that she never pried too much.

Instead, Belasco sorted the cards into three decks, then met Taylor's gaze. "Shall we get started, then?"

Throat tight, Taylor nodded.

"Do you have any specific questions for the cards today?" Belasco asked.

Taylor thought on it. What *was* she here for? They'd "solved" the case already, as much as she didn't believe that. So clearly, personal reasons had brought her in. Inside, she knew what she wanted, but she had a hard time vocalizing it. It was the future she longed to know about. If things would turn out okay.

"I just… want to know about the future," Taylor eventually said. "In a general sense."

With a curt nod, Belasco flipped up the first card. "First, we have The Emperor, reversed. This means tyranny, or coldness, typically associated with a male figure."

Taylor's heart sank. *Like Ben…*

"Next," Belasco said as she flipped up the middle card, "we have The Fool, reversed. This could mean being taken advantage of, or recklessness. Does this mean anything to you?"

Being taken advantage of? No, Taylor was the one who'd taken advantage of Ben by lying to him for so long.

When Taylor didn't respond, Belasco took the hint and continued, flipping up the final card. "Finally, we have The Magician, reversed. This could mean trickery, or illusions." Belasco paused, and her eyes skated over the three cards now face-up on the table.

"Well?" Taylor pressed. "What does it all mean?" She didn't get any of it at all—trickery, being taken advantage of; all it did was make her think of what she'd been doing to Ben. But that had already happened, and she'd confessed—weren't these cards supposed to predict her future, not her past?

"Hmm. I'm getting a strange feeling," Belasco said. "Here, give me your hands."

Taylor hesitated. Despite being more open to the idea of all this fortune telling stuff now, it was still her instinct to question everything. But Belasco blinked at her with her sparkle-lidded eyes, waiting, and Taylor finally handed over her palms. Belasco's smooth, cold palms slid onto Taylor's. Then, she shut her eyes.

Moments passed. Belasco's eyes seemed to be moving back and forth rapidly behind her eyelids, as though she were having a lucid dream. Taylor's heart began to pound as she anticipated Belasco's next move.

Finally, she came in with: "I see… your partner."

Taylor could feel her palms getting sweaty beneath Belasco's. "You mean Ben? My husband?"

Belasco's eyes opened. She retracted her hands, and Taylor wiped her palms on her jeans. "No," Belasco said. "Do you have another partner? Perhaps someone you work with?"

Taylor's stomach dropped. Belasco couldn't be talking about Calvin—could she? He had been acting out of character earlier, which had sounded Taylor's alarm bells. But she trusted Calvin. He was a good partner and a good agent. They'd been through a hell of an ordeal together on their last case, and both had nearly died. But though he'd only been her partner for a short while, Taylor knew that Calvin Scott was rock solid.

But Belasco said, "I sense betrayal. I sense a rash decision, one that might be dangerous."

"I don't understand," Taylor said, trying desperately to puzzle this out. "I do have a partner, but he's good—he wouldn't betray me." *Would he?*

Belasco didn't look convinced. "I can't say for sure the feeling is about him, Mrs. Sage. But there is a strong feeling, and the cards never lie. All I can tell you is what I feel through them, and the visions they gift to me. This partner I sensed doesn't feel romantic. So unless there is anyone else in your life you aren't telling me about, then…"

There was no one else. Taylor had a million more questions. What else was she seeing? What kind of betrayal? But just as she went to blurt them out, her phone began buzzing in her pocket. As much as she wanted to continue this, it could be work, so Taylor abruptly stood from the table. "I have to take this, I'm sorry. It could be work or my husband."

Ducking behind the curtain, Taylor took out her phone.

Calvin Scott's name spread across her screen.

She answered, feeling queasy and distrusting of her partner. *This is ridiculous,* she scolded herself. *The reading must be wrong. Maybe it's about Ben.*

She never thought she'd actually want it to be. Ben, she could work with. But Calvin—a betrayal by him could be potentially life-threatening. In their line of work, trusting your partner was an absolute necessity.

Answering the phone, Taylor said, "Scott, what's going on?"

"Sage, I just got a call from Winchester," Calvin said. His voice was tired. "I need you to come to D.C. Joshua Smith might not be our guy, after all."

"Why?" Taylor's throat tightened. "What happened?"

Calvin sighed. "They found another body."

CHAPTER NINE

Taylor hurried under a barricade of caution tape to a building in downtown D.C., where officers walled the entrance in. Heart pounding, she pulled her badge from her jacket and flashed it to officers as she passed, who promptly allowed her through.

The building's sign had a graphic of an airplane and a luggage carrier, titled BEFORE YOU GO. Calvin hadn't told her much on the phone—only that they'd found another body, and Joshua Smith was most likely not their guy. That was all he could say. Taylor finally reached the front door to the shop, where an officer let her in.

Inside, more cops. And near the back of the store, Calvin stood with his hands on his hips. Taylor hurried over to him. As she approached, the scene appeared over Calvin's shoulder. Taylor's nerves popped and frayed.

The body came into sight. Taylor slowed to a stop.

Slumped against the wall was the body of a young man. A giant splotch of blood pooled through his white shirt underneath his suit jacket, an eerily similar scene to the way Margot Withers had been found.

"Shit," Taylor said, landing beside Calvin.

He barely glanced at her. "Hey, there you are."

"What's going on?" she asked.

"Well, as you can see," Calvin began, "we have another body. Look familiar?"

The slumped position of the body, the single pool of blood on the shirt—it definitely looked like Margot Withers's crime scene. But that didn't make sense. Margot's death felt cold, calculated, planned. More the work of a conspiracy to cover something up. Not the work of a serial killer.

"We're still gathering data," Calvin said, "but the knife pattern seems to match Margot's to a T. A single stab wound with a large blade, potentially a kitchen knife, right to the chest."

A phantom pain struck Taylor's chest as she imagined the scene. She cleared her throat, unsure what to say. If the patterns matched, they had a reason to suspect the cases could be related—but stabbings in

D.C. weren't exactly uncommon, and this could just be random. Taylor needed to know more, so she raised a hand, a signal for the other officers taking photos of the scene to back off so the FBI could get a closer look. The area cleared, and Taylor and Calvin stepped in.

Crouching in front of the body, Taylor took a closer look. The man's eyes were half-open, revealing glassy irises that made her skin crawl. His shirt was ripped in the center of the blood splotch, so he'd clearly been assaulted from the front. But like the last crime scene, there was no blood on the floor. He hadn't been killed here.

Just as Taylor was about to move on, to examine the body again, she noticed a lump in the pocket of his slacks, an oblong shape. Sliding a black glove onto her hand to avoid contaminating the scene, she slowly peered into his pocket.

Inside was a single black chess piece. A horse-shaped knight.

Taylor scowled as she pulled it out and observed it. On the underside was a single white V.

Maybe it was his possession, but it was odd for him to have only one. Maybe it was nothing, but Taylor had that feeling in her gut again that told her this could mean something. If they were dealing with a serial killer, could this chess piece be a token? Though as far as she knew, Margot had not been found with anything like that on her. But she couldn't say for sure until she asked forensics.

Taylor slid the chess piece into an evidence bag and handed it to Calvin as she left the scene, saying, "Be right back—I need to make a phone call."

Finding a quiet corner of the store, next to a poster of an airplane and a happy family traveling, Taylor called the forensics department at Quantico. June Willoughby, a chipper new tech who Taylor had barely interacted with, answered the phone.

"Special Agent Sage, what can I do for you?"

Hugging herself, Taylor leaned toward the wall. "Hey, June, I was hoping you could run something down for me. It's about the Margot Withers's case."

"Sure, what do you need?"

"Was anything significant found on her possession at the time of her death? Actually, I'm looking for something specific—a chess piece."

"Let me check that for you." The sound of a keyboard clacking came from the other end of the phone. "Chess piece, chess piece," June mumbled. "No… no chess piece."

Taylor's heart dropped. Maybe it was insignificant, after all.

Until June said: "Oh, wait! There was no chess *piece,* but there was a chess *sheet."*

Throat tight, Taylor straightened up. "Wait, really?"

"Yep. A chess score sheet. Blank."

There was no way that could be random. It clicked into Taylor's head like the magazine of a gun: there was a connection, and this chess thing was it.

The killer wanted them to find this. She could feel it in her bones

"Thanks, June," Taylor said and hung up, hurrying back over to Calvin, who was still beside the body and looking for clues. He stood up when he saw her, seeming to recognize the look on her face.

"What'd you find out?"

"There was a chess score sheet found on Margot Withers when she died," Taylor said, breathless.

Calvin's brows pinched. "And that evidence bag you gave me…"

"A chess piece. Yeah."

"It could be a connection."

"It has to be," Taylor said. "But we need to know more about our victim."

Taylor glanced down at the body. Outwardly, the only connection she could see between him and Margot were their similar ages, although this man appeared to be closer to his mid-twenties. He was dressed like he could be in politics, but Taylor needed to know for sure. And talking to his family and finding out more about him seemed like the best place to start.

Taylor faced Calvin. "We should go find out more about him, let forensics collect evidence here. If we can find something linking Margot Withers to our new victim…," Taylor paused, her heart becoming swollen in her chest. "Then we might be dealing with a serial killer."

***

The long hallway of an apartment building stretched before Taylor. After doing some recon on the identity of the victim—Liam Stoll—Taylor found out where she and Calvin needed to go. A posh apartment building in downtown D.C., not far from where Liam's body was found. He lived at the end of the hall. Taylor was grateful that this time the police had already informed his grieving widow of his death, so Taylor and Calvin didn't have to be the ones to break the news.

Arriving at apartment 412, Taylor knocked on the door. Calvin was beside her, and he'd been quiet on the drive over. What Belasco had said snuck into her mind—about a partner betraying her. This time, Taylor really didn't want to believe what Belasco had to say. But that didn't ease her feeling of paranoia as she watched Calvin adjust his suit jacket in the corner of her eye.

After several long moments, a woman answered the door. What immediately struck Taylor was that she was dressed business-casual, despite the mascara streaming down her dark cheeks. This was Alissa Stoll, Liam's wife.

"Mrs. Stoll?" Taylor asked as she and Calvin flashed their badges. "We're with the FBI. Do you mind if we come in?"

"I'm assuming this is about Liam." Wiping her eyes with her wrists, she held the door open. "Please come in."

Alissa was clearly trying everything to hold it together, but as Taylor and Calvin stepped into the apartment, Taylor could see the evidence of her grieving: tissue papers on the coffee table and a bottle of red wine, despite it being only five p.m.

"I'm not drunk, if what's what you're thinking," Alissa said, noting that Taylor was staring.

Taylor refocused on her, trying to be respectful. "There would be no judgement if you were. I'm sorry for your loss."

Alissa nodded, giving them a tight-lipped smile, and gestured for them to enter the living room. A second-floor loft rose above, and the apartment gave off an industrial, yet expensive aura. The art on the wall was simple, modern, and classy. Photos of Liam Stoll, alive and smiling, made Taylor's chest lurch.

"Sit wherever you want," Alissa said, taking the recliner chair next to the massive 4K TV. She picked up her glass of wine and took a sip.

Taylor and Calvin exchanged a look. Wiping her palms on her pants, Taylor took the lead. "Once again, I'm sorry for your loss," she said.

Alissa kept her composure. "Do you know who did it?"

"Not yet. We're hoping you can tell us more about your husband—the more we know about him, the closer we may be to finding who was responsible for this."

"Well, where can I even start?" Alissa said. "He was a good guy who didn't deserve this. He dedicated himself to the law, spent most of his time dedicated to law, to defending those in need. And now this." Bitterly, Alissa scoffed, but seemed to catch herself. "Sorry. I'm just angry."

"And you have every right to be," Calvin added in. "It's not fair. We get that."

"And we want nothing more than to put whoever did this behind bars," Taylor said. "The more we understand about Liam, the more we can do that."

"Okay," Alissa replied. "What do you want to know?"

Taylor cleared her throat, unsure how this question would sound. But she couldn't stop thinking about the chess piece. "Was Liam a big chess player?"

Alissa snorted out a laugh. Caught off guard, Taylor frowned. "Sorry," Alissa said, "but no, Liam was not into chess. At all. He was actually tragically bad at it; it was sort of a joke in our friend group. I don't even think he could beat anyone at checkers."

Taylor's pulse increased. That was even less of a reason for Liam to have a chess piece in his pocket.

"What does chess have to do with anything?" Alissa asked.

"It's just a lead we're looking into," Taylor mumbled.

"Well, he was bad at it. But he was good at a lot of other things. Reading people, for one. It made him a great attorney. And if you want to talk about niche interests, Liam was a fencer."

A fencer, Taylor pondered. It didn't seem relevant. And yet something about that information stood out in her mind. As far as she knew, Margot wasn't into anything like that, so that couldn't be the connection.

"You mentioned Liam is an attorney," Calvin said. "Do you think he made any enemies along the way?"

"None that are too dangerous," Alissa said. "He mostly defended the less fortunate. You know, homeless people charged for burglary when they were just looking for a meal. He was that type of person. No, if anything Liam had more friends than enemies. If I could give you his case files, I would."

"Thank you," Calvin said. "We'll need a warrant to access those, if necessary."

Feeling like they had everything, Taylor and Calvin stood up and thanked Alissa for her time. But Taylor couldn't shake what she'd said from her head. The fencing detail.

As she and Calvin left, back into the hallway, it hit her like a bag of bricks.

Liam Stoll was a fencer—a modern day "knight." Which matched his chess piece.

And not only that—Margot Withers, according to Joshua Smith, was viewed as a "pawn."

Taylor's mind raced as she and Calvin walked down the hall, her feet moving on autopilot. Calvin seemed to notice her expression because he said, "Hey, I know that look. You got quiet back there. What are you thinking?"

Still puzzling out the details in her mind, Taylor said, "Liam Stoll was a fencer. Like a knight. And Margot Withers was a pawn."

Calvin blinked for a moment, before he mused, "A knight and a pawn."

"Exactly. But what does it all mean?" Her thoughts raced so fast that she could barely keep up. Theories beckoned to bloom, but she couldn't quite put her finger on them. Taylor didn't know much about chess. It was something that Ben liked, and she obviously couldn't ask him. "Scott," Taylor said, "if we're going to catch this guy before he claims another victim, then we need to figure out this chess angle. I don't suppose it's something you're into?"

"Nah, not my thing…," Calvin looked up for a moment, like he was deep in thought. "But now that I think about it, there's an old buddy of mine who may actually be able to help us here. The guy's a mega chess nerd."

"Can you set up a meeting?"

"Of course." Calvin took out his phone and searched through his contacts, making the call. Taylor stepped away to give him some privacy, pacing down the hallway of the building.

If she hadn't been sure that it was a serial killer before—she definitely was now.

CHAPTER TEN

Taylor had never stepped foot in a chess club before, but as she and Calvin entered, she was surprised by how populated it was. It was a small, cramped space with dim lighting, but tables upon tables of chessboards made up a grid in the room, almost all occupied with different men and women facing off against each other. Vending machines were set up along the back wall, and a stand selling chess boards and merch for the club was erected along the right side of the room. It was like a bar for chess players.

Following behind Calvin, Taylor eyed the back of his suit jacket. She hadn't been able to shake away her paranoid thoughts about him on the ride over. This wasn't the first time Belasco had gotten in her head, but she had to believe that this time, the fortune teller was wrong. During the Jeremiah Swanson case, Taylor never doubted Calvin's integrity for a second. What could he possibly betray her over? It didn't make sense.

And besides, what extent of "betrayal" had Belasco seen? Maybe it was minor; maybe he'd forget to get her a coffee and that'd be the betrayal.

Or maybe it could be something huge. Life-altering. He was her partner, after all—there would be times when their lives were in each other's hands, so absolute trust was essential.

So how can I prove she's wrong? Do I test him somehow?

It all sounded silly. Maybe it would be better if she just told him the truth.

Taylor inwardly groaned as she imagined how insane she'd look. *"Hey, Scott, I went to a fortune teller and her cards told me you were going to betray me and now I'm terrified. Can you refute that please?"*

She cringed away. That was never going to happen.

Refocusing on the case, Taylor snapped from her thoughts as she and Calvin approached a front desk. A handsome man, probably around Calvin's age, with a trim plaid shirt approached them with a wide smile. He wore thick-rimmed glasses, but aside from that, he didn't look like the stereotypical portrayal of a chess champion—more like someone Taylor would see at a hipster bar over an IPA.

"Calvin Scott, is that really you?" He approached with his arms wide open.

"Hey, Carter," Calvin said with a laugh. The two hugged, and Carter patted him on the back like they were old friends.

"And this must be your partner." Carter's blue eyes were magnified by his glasses. He held out a hand, and Taylor reluctantly shook it. "I'm Carter Cohen, but I'm sure Calvin already gave you the run-down on me. Most people just call me Double C. With Calvin, we were triple."

Actually, he'd barely said a word on the drive up, just that Carter was an old friend and a big player in the chess community. A sizzle of suspicion regrew in Taylor. It wasn't like Calvin to be so quiet, and the longer it dragged on, the more paranoid she became.

After all, Belasco had been right before.

Stop. You're being ridiculous.

"Uh, yeah," Taylor said. "Special Agent Taylor Sage. Nice to meet you."

"Can we go somewhere more private?" Calvin glanced around the room.

"Of course, man, follow me," Carter said.

They followed him to a room that had a table and a vending machine in it. Carter sat on one side of the table, Taylor and Calvin on the other.

"Sorry we don't have much time to catch up," Calvin said. "Truth is, we're working a case right now, and things took a weird turn."

"Must be weird if you're coming to me," Carter said, clasping his hands on the table. "What can I help with?"

Calvin glanced at Taylor, as if signaling her to take the lead. She obliged and began explaining the case in as much detail as she was allowed to.

"We have two bodies so far," she said. "The first victim was related to the world of politics, and we initially had a solid theory as to why she was targeted. But the second victim is when things took a turn. He had no relation to politics, from what we can see. And not only that, but we found this in his pocket."

Taylor showed Carter a photo of the chess piece in its evidence bag—the black knight.

"At first," Taylor said, "the only connection was that both victims appeared to have been killed in a similar manner. That wasn't enough to say the cases were related. Until we found this on the first victim."

Taylor showed Carter a photo of the chess score sheet, which was blank. Forensics had sent it to Taylor earlier, along with any other photos that could be relevant.

Carter's brows stitched as he observed the sheet. "Interesting. I haven't seen that particular sheet before, although it could be generic." He sat back, thinking. "So you guys are thinking this could be a serial killer, and he's using the chess-related tokens to send some sort of message?"

"Yes," Taylor said. "Victim one had been described as a 'pawn.' Victim two was very into fencing, which relates him to being a 'knight'—which also matches the piece found on him."

"That does seem significant," Carter agreed.

"We won't know for sure it's a serial killer until we see a third victim," Calvin said, "but obviously, my partner and I would rather skip that part."

"Of course." Carter sat back and crossed his hands behind his head.

Silence befell them as he seemed to be thinking up a response. Taylor glanced at Calvin in her periphery. Another intrusive thought penetrated her mind, telling her to be wary of Calvin—maybe wary of his friend too.

Stop, she scolded herself. This wasn't like her. Since when was she paranoid? She made a mental note to talk to her dad about it. He was a psychologist, after all. But she didn't know how to tell him without confessing she'd been seeing a fortune teller, which she knew he'd frown upon. Taylor was the same way before the Swanson case. In a way, she wished she was still like that.

If she still believed fortune telling and tarot was all bullshit, then she wouldn't have these distracting thoughts swimming through her head.

Finally, Carter spoke. "This might be a longshot, and totally unfounded," he said. "The last thing I want to do is throw an innocent person under the bus. But I will say, the timing of this is a bit interesting."

Taylor sat up, listening intently. Her heart thrummed as she waited for Carter to come out with it. If he had an actual lead—they needed to know it. Now. The last thing Taylor wanted was for another body to drop. It'd be last time all over again—that horrible loss of control as somebody stole life after life, and Taylor was unable to stop it.

"There's this guy," Carter said. "Not even two weeks ago, he was kicked out of the club. He was a real pro, one of the best players I've ever seen. He gave me a run for my money more than a few times… but we found out he was cheating."

"Cheating how?" Taylor asked.

"He was wearing an earpiece. He had a friend monitor the games and helping him come up with strategies. The friend was a real smart guy, and George—that's his name, George Fields—had been paying him to help out and keep his mouth shut. Now, none of us know how much of George's game was the other guy, and how much was really his. Either way, his earpiece fell out during one of the matches and he got caught quick. Kicking him out was messy. He threatened to kick all our asses. It wasn't a surprise, really—we'd heard from one of his ex-girlfriend's that George had a temper and a history of getting into bar fights."

George sounded mildly promising, or at least, worthy of questioning. With him having a history of violence, and recently being expelled from the club, there could be a connection. But Taylor didn't understand how he chose his victims; she would think George would be looking to enact revenge on those who betrayed him directly, not random people. Still, they had no other leads to go with, so it was either track down George or go home and call it a night. And the last thing Taylor wanted was to go home to Ben.

"Do you know where George is now?" Taylor asked.

"Not sure where he lives, but last I heard, he'd started up a tournament in Dupont Circle at this park called Four Acres. They have matches there all the time—George's entire life revolves around chess. If you're lucky, you might even catch him there now."

Taylor stood. They had their answers. "Thank you, Carter. This has been extremely valuable."

Calvin stood too and offered Carter a hand. "Thanks, buddy. We'll let you know if anything comes out of his."

"Happy to help, guys. I hope you catch whoever's doing it."

Taylor thanked Carter again, then she and Calvin exited the chess club, onto the D.C. street and to Calvin's car. Calvin got into the driver's seat, and Taylor slid into the passenger side, still feeling vaguely anxious from her invasive thoughts about Belasco. As she settled into the car with Calvin, he started it up and began driving.

"So," he said, "what'd you think of Carter?"

Taylor glanced at him as he drove. "He seems good. How do you two know each other?"

A nostalgic smile took over Calvin's face. "Actually, we went to college together." He shot her a smirk, seeming more like the Calvin she knew, which helped her relax a little. "Once upon a time, Sage, I actually wanted to go into computer science. That's Carter's field."

"Wait, you almost weren't an agent?" Taylor asked, surprised. He was a bit dorky at times, but she couldn't picture him as anything else.

"Yep," he said. "I went into computer science, and that's where I met Carter. But I'd always had an interest in law. I didn't think I'd be any good, though. To be honest, when I was a kid, I wasn't really good at anything."

Taylor watched him as he spoke while driving, listening intently. She didn't know much of Calvin's backstory, but she appreciated him opening up—it was more than she'd given him in the short time they'd known each other. Although, of course, Calvin knew a bit more about her and Ben than she would have liked.

"Anyway," he said, "while I was there for computers, I actually sort of accidentally uncovered some crime that was happening on campus. Turned out there was actually a mini 'dark web' going around, where guys at school would trade nudes of their girlfriends—some of them underage."

Taylor recoiled in disgust. "That's horrible," she said.

And all too common, unfortunately. Colleges and universities could be a cesspool of crime, particularly sexual crimes against young women. It was a breeding ground for hormones and alcohol, so it was no surprise some people lost control. This interval of calculated crime Calvin was describing, though, was another thing entirely.

Taylor thought back to her own time in the FBI Academy. She was lucky to say she'd had a clean experience. Maybe being surrounded by aspiring agents kept everyone in line, although she also knew that wasn't always the case. Even law officers could break the law, after all. People were just people.

"It was," Calvin continued. "Carter and I ended up sort of teaming up to track down who was behind it. Turns out it was this jock-type guy. We hacked his computer and sent everything anonymously to the cops." A wistful smile crossed his lips. "Honestly, I'd never felt so alive. From then on out, computers weren't enough for me. I was never really good with them anyway." Their eyes met. "I dropped out. From there, the FBI caught my eye, and I worked my way into the FBI Academy. And, well, here I am."

"It's quite the leap," Taylor commented.

"Yeah, and I worked my ass off for it," he said. "I know you did too."

It was true. The FBI Academy had been one of the biggest hurdles of her career—second only to actually working as an FBI agent, which was obviously extremely taxing on the body, mind, and soul. But despite everything, Taylor wouldn't have it any other way.

"I think you made the right decision," Taylor said. "I can't picture you as anything else, Scott. The FBI suits you."

"Thanks, Sage." He focused on the road as he drove, and Taylor considered his story.

Calvin Scott was a good guy. He was long before he met her, and he would continue to be, no matter where he ended up in life. Maybe she did still feel paranoid about him, but they had a case to work—and he was still her partner, so she would keep her professionalism up.

It was time to refocus on the case. Next destination: Dupont Circle. George Fields had potential—but Taylor really hoped she wasn't walking into another dead end.

CHAPTER ELEVEN

It was just before sunset when Taylor and Calvin arrived at Dupont Circle and left their car in a parking lot across the street. Taylor figured there was only a good hour of sunlight left, which meant if there was an outdoor chess tournament going on, it would probably end soon.

At least it was warm out—a mild breeze blew in as Taylor and Calvin trekked toward Four Acres Park, which seemed to have a crowd gathered near it. In truth, this lead was flimsy—Taylor felt a bit like a chicken running around with her head chopped off. Why would George Fields kill Margot Withers and Liam Stoll if it was Carter's chess club that he was angry with? The motivation didn't quite line up, but the connection to chess and the timing did make this worth looking into. It was better than nothing.

As they drew closer to the park, tables came into sight. An arching sign hung over the park entrance, reading FOUR ACRES PARK. A cardboard sign was set up near the entrance, which read: CHESS CLUB TOURNY TODAY! ALL ARE WELCOME!

"Seems pleasant enough," Taylor said.

Calvin hadn't spoken much since they left Carter's. "Bet they don't know they're organizer could be a violent, cheating psychopath," he commented.

The way his voice was full of disdain at the word "cheating" reassured Taylor. Because cheating is a betrayal, and surely, Calvin didn't think betrayals were a good look.

I need to get this out of my damn head.

Trying to stay in the present, Taylor focused on entering the park with Calvin. They would need a reason to be there, and based on what Carter said, George Fields might not play nice. Taylor realized they hadn't gone over their game plan yet. Time was running out, so she stopped Calvin beside a bench, right before the park's archway-shaped entrance.

"I don't think a direct approach is our best bet with this guy," she said. "He sounds unhinged, potentially violent."

Calvin scanned the park. "Agreed. We don't wanna freak him out with badges. What's your gut instinct?"

Taylor's eyes skated over to the table by the entrance, which had papers all over it and people sitting behind it wearing matching blue shirts. That must have been the sign-up table.

An unusual—and potentially insane—idea popped into her head. She wanted to interact with George Fields in his element. See how he was naturally. And according to Carter, there was no better element to catch him in than during a game of chess.

"I think I should play him in a game," Taylor said. It sounded stupid, even to her, but it was the brightest idea she had.

Calvin cocked an eyebrow. "You a closeted chess pro, Sage? Because don't look at me. I'm more of a video game guy."

She chewed her lip. The last time she'd played chess was with her dad when she was fourteen. Angie had liked board games. When she disappeared, the family sort of stopped talking about them. The memory of her family at the dinner table, laughing as Angie and Taylor had faced off against each other in chess, made her stomach roll.

"No, I'm not," Taylor muttered. Then—another idea. If George Fields had gotten away with cheating for so long, then maybe Taylor could take some inspiration from the man himself. "But what if we take a play from Fields's own book?" she suggested.

Calvin shifted his weight, hands in the pockets of his slacks. "I'm listening…"

"That new girl in tech, June Willoughby—she said she likes chess."

It clued in on Calvin's face. He nodded with a sly smile. "You're always thinking ahead, Sage. Let's get her on the phone."

***

Taylor secured the earpiece and undid her ponytail so her long, black hair covered it. She stopped right before the entrance to the park, where it looked like they were still accepting sign-ups. In her ear, June's voice came through:

"Special Agent Sage, can you hear me?"

"Yeah, I can hear you," Taylor muttered, turning to Calvin so it looked like she was talking to him. Taylor whispered, "Once more, here's the plan: Agent Scott will keep track of the board and relay that information to you. Then you'll let me know which move I should make. I don't need to win, but I need to buy enough time to question the guy without seeming too suspicious."

"Roger that," June said. "And don't worry. You'll win."

Taylor could practically hear the wink in June's voice. She was starting to like this girl.

Without any further distractions, Taylor strode up to the sign-up table, Calvin behind her. A short girl holding a clipboard greeted them and smiled like a chipmunk.

"Hi, folks! Are you here to watch or play?"

"Play," Taylor said, acting casual. "Does George Fields happen to be here?"

"Oh, yes, George is in a match right now."

Taylor looked around but didn't recognize him among the sea of faces. She had looked up George's file on the way here; he had a minor criminal record, after all, and his mugshot had looked like an overweight man with a sunken face. There were a few people here who could match that description.

"Sorry, where is he?" Taylor asked. "I forgot my glasses…"

"Right over there, red shirt," the girl said.

Taylor zeroed in on him. A heavyset man in a bright red polo shirt, glasses, and balding hair leaned over the table. *Got you,* Taylor thought. If he was wearing an earpiece, it wasn't obvious. George made a move, snapping a piece across the board—and clearly, he won the game, because he stood up and made dramatic gestures in the air. Not exactly a humble winner.

"That's great." Taylor faced the girl eagerly. "I've heard George is the best player around. I really wanted a chance to play him."

"Oh, well…" The girl checked her clipboard. "I think he's already set up to match against someone next, but—"

"Someone wants to play against me?" a male voice interrupted.

Taylor turned to see George standing right behind her—a little too close. A vague smell of sausage wafted off him. A gross smirk laced his mouth, and Taylor's stomach churned. She immediately got a creepy vibe from George. A killer, maybe or maybe not—but the way he glanced up her body definitely told her he was a pervert. It didn't seem to matter if Taylor was wearing long sleeves and pants, leaving much room for the imagination. A feeling of disgust moved in her gut.

But for the case, she had to push through it and get close to this guy.

"Uh, yeah, hi…" She cleared her throat, averting her stare. "I heard you're the best around, so I wanted to—"

"You got it, girly," George said. "C'mon, let's get started. It's not every day I'm directly challenged. By a pretty lady, no less."

Taylor wanted to vomit. She glanced over to see where Calvin was—he had distanced himself enough to look like a stranger, but locked eyes with her to show he was still following. She gave him a subtle nod before she followed George over to the picnic table, where the chess board was set up. A small crowd of spectators already waited. Calvin distanced himself from them, still staying close enough to get a view of the board.

By now, the sun was setting, creating a warm hue over the park. Sitting down across from George at the picnic table, Taylor's palms were sweaty. The sight of the chess board had her mind reeling. She had no clue what she was doing. But June's voice appeared again:

"Sage, Scott says you're about to start. I'm here. You've got this. I'll take your silence as a 'hell yeah.'"

Taylor resisted a laugh; never in her life had she said, "hell yeah."

"Scott says you're white, which means you go first," June said.

Across from Taylor, George was breathing heavily, eyeing her beneath his thin-rimmed glasses. "Your move, madam," he said.

"Move your third piece from the right—your pawn—forward."

Taylor did as she was told.

Across from her, George made the same move.

"He's probably going to make it seem like he's mirroring you for a while," June said. "Don't fall for it. You two are probably going to fight for the center."

June instructed Taylor on her next move, and so she slid another piece. George did the same thing, watching her. They only had so much time before the match would be over, so Taylor knew she had to start asking the questions fast.

"So, George," Taylor began. "How long have you been playing chess?"

"Oh, probably since before you were born," he droned on. "My dad taught me, and his dad taught him, and so on… it's a family thing. How did you hear about me?"

Taylor thought on her next move—not in the game, June was telling her what to do there. But the approach to George was all on her, and as much as she hated it, it seemed like he wanted her to be flirty. There hadn't been many cases in Taylor's career where she was willing to stoop to that level, and she wasn't about to now. But a bit of ego-floating could go a long way here. Taylor put her pride aside and played along.

"You're a bit of a local legend, don't you know?" she said and moved another piece.

George did the same. "Of course I know."

As June predicted, they were "fighting for the center."

June said, "His plays are unpredictable… he's good. But I'm better. Move your knight forward."

Taylor did as she was told. She didn't fully understand if or how she was winning, but she trusted June's judgement. George's face reddened as he watched the board, taking longer than he did before to make a move. He was getting flustered.

Time to dig deeper.

"Do you normally prefer black?" Taylor asked, thinking about the black knight piece that had been found on Liam Stoll's body.

"Usually," George said shortly. He made a quick move. June instructed Taylor's next, and she did so, taking out one of George's pieces. His scowl was growing deeper.

"Is there a reason?" Taylor asked. "Some people prefer to go first."

"A first move can indicate a lot about your opponent, and I like to stay ahead. But you…"

George scowled up at her and made a move. June was quick with her instructions, and Taylor made another one, snagging another one of his pieces.

By this point, George's face matched the bright red of his shirt. His beady eyes peered at her. "What's going on here? No one's come this close to beating me all day." He leaned in, looking closer, and closer.

Taylor tried to turn away—but it was too late.

George's stubby hand reached out and snagged the earpiece from her. He must have seen it, and panic surged through Taylor. George abruptly stood, nearly knocking over the picnic table, and Taylor scrambled to her feet to get away.

"Cheater!" George screeched. The people around them gasped. Before Taylor could react, George dove right over the table, knocking over the chess board, his hands reaching for her. She ducked away, but he managed to grab her shoulders and shake her hard, screaming, "Cheater!" over and over again.

Taylor kneed him in the gut, and he quickly keeled over. She went to regain her balance, but George scrambled up to his feet again and charged her.

“You think you can make a fool out of me, bitch!?” He dove at her again, but Taylor dodged out of the way, sending George falling face-first to the grass.

By now, Calvin was running up to them. But Taylor took her chance while George’s belly was flat on the ground and climbed onto his back, pinning him down. His weight was tremendous, and when he tried to stand, he knocked her back. Calvin arrived just in time to take over—he forced George to the ground. It became a team effort as Taylor came in with the cuffs. Calvin twisted George’s hands behind his back, and he growled in pain as Taylor cuffed him.

“George Fields, you just assaulted a federal agent,” Taylor said. “You have the right to remain silent.”

She had to admit—getting a win on this guy felt like a win for her too.

CHAPTER TWELVE

George Fields now sat across from Taylor again—this time, on the other side of an interrogation room table at a police station in D.C., and she had Calvin right beside her. Taylor had questioned so many people in her life that she felt she'd probably seen it all—but George Fields was a new one, even to her.

She had never dealt with anyone so condescending in her life.

"You two are pathetic," George spat, rattling in his chair. He was handcuffed to prevent him from attacking anyone again. Taylor and Calvin remained quiet as he ranted on and on. "You think you're so smart because you hide behind guns and badges—you probably have the intellect of a common chimp! You could never beat me without cheating, you—you—" Flustered, George stopped himself, rattling his cuffs like a pig racking against the walls of his pen. He grunted in frustration.

This man was pathetic. They'd been in the interrogation room for a total of five minutes now and he'd done nothing but rant. Taylor hoped he'd eventually run out of steam and start answering some questions, but his plump red face showed no signs of slowing down.

Taylor considered her options for getting him to talk. She definitely didn't feel like playing nice, and now that all George's power had been robbed, she didn't feel the need to. Time to push his buttons and see what she could get out.

"Funny you say that," Taylor said, crossing her arms, "because we know you were removed from your last chess club due to cheating."

George's face went steely. "Lies. A conspiracy. All of it. I never cheated. Those fuckers made that up." His fists balled up, his rage peaking by the second.

Well, that confirmed the truth behind Carter's words—that George had a vendetta against the club. But again, neither Margot Withers nor Liam Stoll had any connection to the world of chess. If George had wanted to enact revenge on anybody, would it not have been Carter and his club directly?

Taylor sighed and opened up the file before her on the table. She took out two photos: one of the chess sheet that was found on Margot

Withers, the other of the chess piece found on Liam Stoll. She slid them across the table, and George's beady brown eyes flitted to them. He didn't react.

"What am I supposed to do with this?" he asked.

"Do you recognize these items, George?" Taylor inquired.

"Do I look like a fool?" George countered. "It's a knight and a chess score sheet. As a professional chess player, you can easily infer I would know all about these. Don't insult me."

"These *specific* pieces?" Taylor pressed. Unless George was a master manipulator—which Taylor doubted—he wouldn't be able to hold himself together for long before cracking.

"What game are you two small-minded fools playing?" His eyes flitted between Taylor and Calvin. "Are you suggesting I used those to cheat or something? Those images mean nothing to me."

Taylor narrowed her eyes, observing George for any sign of deceit. As much as she hated to admit it—he didn't seem like a cold-blooded killer. And the motive still didn't make sense. But to be sure, Taylor asked, "Where were you on August 30th?"

"Chess club. All day and all night."

"What chess club?" Calvin asked, speaking for the first time in a while.

George held up his nose and snorted. "Carter's isn't the only place in D.C. I've begun renting my own building. I fail to see what this has to do with anything."

"Does this building have security cameras?" Taylor asked.

"Of course it does. I need to keep an eye on anyone who might be cheating." George's eyes flared on Taylor. "You would know all about that, cheater."

Taylor resisted rolling her eyes. "And what about the 20th?"

George heaved out a sigh, like being here was an inconvenience to him. "Chess club during the day. Chess tournament at night in the park. Chess, chess, chess. That's all I do. Do you know what the definition of insanity is? Doing the same thing over and over and expecting a different result. You can ask me what I was doing all you want, and I'll give you the same answers: I was playing chess. Or eating dinner."

It took everything in Taylor not to respond to George's aggravating rant. Taylor jotted his alleged alibis down in her file. They would definitely look into them—but in all honesty, she had a feeling George would check out. This was likely nothing but another dead-end.

Damn it. More wasted time.

“What’s really going on here?” George asked. “Do you expect me to believe the FBI would be interested in a cheating scandal—a totally *untrue* cheating scandal—within the chess community? And what do those arbitrary dates mean?”

“Surely a smart guy like you could’ve picked up on it by now,” Calvin said.

Taylor glanced at him. She didn’t mind the moxie, but Calvin was usually more compassionate than sarcastic. Her suspicions arose again from earlier, Beslaco’s words playing like a ticking time bomb in her head. When would it explode and reveal the truth?

“Do elaborate,” George said.

Closing her file, Taylor faced him. “We’re investigating two murders that seem to be connected by the two images I showed you.”

The color drained from George’s flushed face. “*What now?*”

“You heard her,” Calvin said. “Murders. As in, real people are dead. And you’re looking pretty suspicious right now, so I’d cut the attitude.”

“What?” George shook his head violently. “Oh, no you don’t! I had nothing to do with any murders—there are cameras all over my building, and witnesses, people who can vouch for me. I did *not* murder anyone.”

Of course, knowing the stakes were so high changed his tune, which only amplified Taylor’s gut instinct that George wasn’t their guy. But even if that were the case—he was clearly still extremely involved in the world of chess. Maybe he could prove useful. Trying to validate his own innocence may light a fire under his ass to name anyone who could be a potential suspect.

“Calm down, George,” Taylor said. “We will verify your whereabouts on the nights of the murders. But if you know anything about the pictures I showed you—or who could be responsible for this—then we would suggest you tell us.”

George smacked his lips as he took in a ragged breath. “Let me see them again,” he stammered.

Taylor slid the photos across the table again. George greedily leaned over. So much sweat had pooled on his forehead that it dripped down onto the table. Taylor scowled in disgust. He continued to smack his lips, breathing heavily as he examined the photos with bulging eyes.

“Uh, um—the knight, well, I can’t tell you anything about it based on just a picture. But…” He leaned closer to the chess score sheet. “You know. I know a guy who uses this exact sheet.”

Taylor leaned forward. Her pulse thumped. This was leading somewhere. She had hoped George might have some insight, but he actually knew somebody who used this specific sheet? She anxiously said, "Who, George?"

His eyes eagerly found Taylor's. "Hans Stender. He's this real weird German guy, a custom chess piece maker. He's got a shop in D.C. We order from him all the time. But he's truly an antisocial guy. Very weird. Even among chess players."

Antisocial, strange, and uses the exact same chess sheet? Taylor checked her watch. There was barely any light left in the day—but since they were still in D.C., there was a chance they could make it to Hans's shop just in time to catch him.

Taylor and Calvin stood, having obtained all they needed, and headed toward the door.

"Wait, what's gonna happen to me!?" George shouted. "I didn't hurt anyone! You have to let me out!"

Taylor stopped before the door and looked over her shoulder at the pathetic man restrained in the chair. "We'll verify that," she said before she left the room, leaving George Fields to sit there and think about the choices in his life that had led him to this moment.

Taylor had dealt with a lot of foul men in her life, but he was definitely up there. She just hoped this brush with the law would steer him in the right direction—although she doubted it.

She and Calvin reconvened outside of the interrogation room. They watched George as he squirmed on the other side of the glass.

"Well, that was awful," Calvin said with a sigh. "What do you think? Do we believe him?"

"I don't know," Taylor admitted. "I have to be honest; Fields's motivations for the murders don't add up to me. You'd think if he wanted to hurt anyone, it would be Carter and the others at his chess club. However, he's definitely a piece of shit, and he did assault me, so he belongs here."

"Yeah, I could see that. So what about this Stender guy?"

Taylor pivoted toward the door. "I think you know what I'm going to say, Scott." She held open the door. "If we get going now, we might be able to catch him."

Calvin sighed with a laugh and followed after. "I wouldn't have you any other way, Sage. Let's get him."

CHAPTER THIRTEEN

The entrance to Hans Stender's custom chess shop loomed above Taylor as Calvin stood beside her, hands in the pockets of his slacks. The sun was just setting, and long shadows stretched over the east side of D.C. An OPEN sign hung on the other side of the glass, but the hours sheet below it said the shop closed at six p.m., and it was ten after.

Still, Taylor had every intention of going in. She had gone over the plan with Calvin on the way over—a direct approach sounded best, as according to George Fields's description, Stender was antisocial and cagey. He probably wouldn't talk much without a fire under him. And the FBI knocking on his shop's door had to be enough to get him to open up.

Calvin opened the door to the shop, holding it for Taylor. She passed under his arm as the bell rang. Inside, it was dark and cramped—a dim light radiated from the back of the store behind the register, providing just enough light to illuminate the glassy shelves that surrounded them. Everything looked expensive—chess board upon chess board was placed on each shelf. As Taylor stepped farther into the store, she saw some of the back shelves held individual pieces. Some were large, others were tiny. But they all appeared finely crafted. A scent of sawdust hung in the air.

It was a beautiful shop, Taylor had to admit. Very well put together. At the same time, something felt off here. It was almost *too* clean. And there were so many products; did anyone even come in here to shop?

"Who are you?"

A sudden voice caused both Taylor and Calvin to startle. Before they could react, a tall, lithe man slithered out from the shadows. The crooked light in the shop accentuated the wrinkles on his deep-set face, and he was wiping his hands off with a towel. Dust pieces—or maybe chips of wood—splattered his clothing.

"I didn't have any appointments scheduled," the man said. He spoke with a thick German accent.

This had to be Hans Stender himself. Taylor had every intention of showing her badge, but first, she wanted to gage him a little more before dropping the bomb.

"Do people normally only come in with appointments?" Taylor asked. It seemed odd, for such a small, niche shop to not welcome every potential customer with open arms. A tinge of fear grew in Taylor—if Hans really was their guy, he probably wouldn't go down without a fight. He wasn't particularly built, but he was abnormally tall. The last time Taylor had dealt with such a tall perp, it had been Jeremiah Swanson, and he'd nearly killed both her and Calvin.

Taylor took comfort in the weight of her gun on her belt, hidden beneath her blazer.

Hans's face was grim. "Not many people come by… are you hoping to buy something? Perhaps come back tomorrow—I am very busy in the workshop. Schedule an appointment and we can talk." Hans gestured toward the door. "Now, if you please…"

Clearly, he wasn't budging. Taylor pulled out her badge, and Calvin did the same. Hans's scowl deepened, leathery face becoming more wrinkled.

"What is this?" he asked.

"We're with the FBI," Taylor said. "I'm Special Agent Taylor Sage, and this is my partner, Agent Calvin Scott. Do you mind if we ask you a few questions?"

"Questions about what?" Hans asked sternly. "What is this about? I really am busy."

Not immediately cooperating was a red flag. Calvin seemed to agree, because he said, "We're investigating a series of crimes that we think may be linked to the world of chess. We were hoping you could help us out. As a custom chess maker, you clearly know your stuff."

While Hans's expression was still dark, he nodded, tucking his rag into the pocket of his jeans. "What do you want to know?"

A lot of things, Taylor thought. She decided to start simple.

"How long have you been in business?" she asked.

"For over thirty years," Hans said. "As soon as I moved to America, I started my shop. We have been here ever since."

"You said 'we,'" Taylor noted. "Do you have employees?"

"No, it is just me."

"No wife? A co-owner?"

Hans shook his head.

Taylor observed him. He had been all alone here for thirty years? Not a single employee, no partner—more flags were building up. Taylor had seen time and time again the way these loner types tended to snap, sometimes on people who they idealized. Margot Withers and Liam Stoll were both young and attractive with their whole lives ahead of them. Could Hans Stender have coveted that?

It wouldn't have been the first case she'd worked where an older, homelier person had become fascinated with youth—and taking it away. The obsession with beauty was seen time and time again. Taylor could speculate all she wanted—but she needed to know more before drawing any conclusions. The chess score sheet was enough of a link to put Hans high up on the potential suspect list, especially if the sheet was unique.

Still, there was nothing to prove it yet. They only had George Fields's word, and he was barely credible. Maybe if Taylor actually *found* the sheet in the shop, she'd have a sound reason to bring him in. Hearsay wasn't enough.

"Well, it's a really beautiful shop," Taylor said. "Do you mind if we take a look around?"

Hans's posture seemed to shrink. Now, he was showing nerves. "Well...," his large Adam's apple bobbed. "Go ahead. But please do not touch anything. Everything is extremely fragile and expensive. I make everything myself."

Taylor made no promises; she had every intention of touching an item or two, but of course she wouldn't intentionally destroy his shop. With that, she began moving through the store. She took one side while Calvin took the other. It was a bit hard to see with the half-light, but Taylor knew what she was looking for—she spent some time pretending to observe the chess boards before she systematically made her way toward the back of the shop.

There was a window behind the cash register that led to a brighter room that Taylor could only assume was the workshop. Without asking, she moved past the register. By this time, Calvin was right there with her again. They casually strolled toward the back room.

And Hans was right behind them.

"This way leads to my workshop," he muttered. "It is private."

Taylor gave him a stiff, forced smile. "We'll just take a quick look." It was not a request.

Thankfully, Hans didn't resist, but Taylor could tell this was driving him crazy. His brow twitched and a redness took over his face.

On top of that, he was holding his hands together so tightly it looked like they would break.

Something to hide, Stender?

The workshop was small, but a lightbulb hung from the ceiling, giving it much more light than the rest of the shop. There was a worktable with a stool and a cabinet full of tiny tools used for carving out the intricate details on the chess pieces. On the table, a half-made chess piece waited to be finished. Next to it was black paint. So, he hand-painted all of these? That must have taken a lot of patience—and meticulous detail. Taylor thought of the stab wounds on the two victims; how each had a single, clean stab, no unnecessary tearing in their clothing. It, too, was meticulously done.

After poking around the workshop, though, Taylor found nothing unusual. Calvin gave her a shrug. Maybe it was time to whip out the evidence photos, step this up a notch. But something in Taylor's gut told her to come up with an excuse to keep looking. They needed that sheet.

"Let's head back out to the main shop," Taylor said. "We're almost done, Mr. Stender."

She avoided Hans's suspicious eyes as she and Calvin breezed past him, back into shop. And that was when Taylor realized—she hadn't looked behind the cash register. On the table surrounding it, she noticed a stack of papers beside a glass display case of small, delicate-looking chess pieces.

Taylor's heart pounded as she drew near.

It was a stack of chess score sheets like the one found on Margot Withers. But she needed to get closer to make sure they were an exact match.

As she went to go pick one of the papers up, her elbow knocked the small display case. The chess pieces in it rattled. One of them fell over, and on instinct, Taylor went to pick it up and put it back.

"Don't touch those!" Hans shouted, storming over.

But when he saw Taylor already had one of his pieces in her hand, a look of pure anger devoured his expression. Taylor had seen that look before—animalistic rage. It always came before an attack. She didn't have a moment to react before Hans Stender shoved her, and she went toppling back—right onto a massive glass chess board that was set up against the wall.

The strength shocked her. The sound of shattering glass screamed against her ears, and she felt it all break beneath her weight.

But the pain that followed shocked her more.

Hot, searing pain scorched her arm, and Taylor looked down, feeling out of her body as she realized a massive piece of glass was protruding from her arm, and there was blood. *Everywhere.*

She became queasy, her head featherlight. Still in shock, Taylor dared to look up. She became dizzy. The room spun. *No, no, not again!*

She didn't want to lose consciousness—if she did, Calvin would be alone. Maybe he couldn't take Stender. He was big, just like Jeremiah Swanson had been big. But Taylor was in shock. She couldn't move a muscle.

Through her hazy vision, she saw Calvin rush at Stender. Stender shoved him back, using his height to his advantage. But Calvin quickly regained his composure and pulled out his gun, pointing it right at Stender, who threw his hands up.

"That's right, now put your hands behind your back!" Calvin demanded, still holding that gun.

Stender, trembling, did as he was told. Calvin strapped cuffs on him and shoved him to the floor, still holding his gun.

"Do *not* move," he demanded.

Then, Calvin rushed over to Taylor. Her consciousness was returning, but the initial wound had thrown her back in time for a moment. Not wanting to appear weak, she went to stand as Calvin reached her, helping her up. Her weight wobbled against him. But they won; the realization sent relief through her. Calvin got him. Though the pain continued to throb, Taylor was able to relax, just for a moment.

"Sage, Jesus," Calvin said as he observed her arm. "We need to get you to a hospital now."

Taylor looked down at her wound, still gushing blood, and became lightheaded again—then suddenly, her body weakened.

Everything went white.

CHAPTER FOURTEEN

After her last visit, Taylor had never wanted to step foot in another hospital again. But here she was, lying on a sickly white bed, wincing as the doctor stitched the flesh on her forearm—in and out, in and out. She had to admit, it was mesmerizing to watch.

"You're lucky, Mrs. Sage," the nurse said. She was young and must've been fresh out of college. Taylor flinched again as another stich sewed shut her arm. Taylor would barely call this "lucky"—she'd lost consciousness back at Stender's, only to wake up here. But the nurse continued, "A few inches over and this would've hit a main artery, and we'd have a way bigger problem on our hands."

Okay, maybe she was a little lucky. But getting hurt badly on the job was embarrassing for her. Taylor didn't like being the victim; it went against every part of her nature. She was supposed to be the one who saved, not the one who *got* saved.

The nurse finished the final stitch, cut the string, and looked at Taylor with a smile. "That should just about do it."

"Thanks," Taylor muttered, lifting and observing her arm. The scar was nasty, and the thick black stitching didn't make it look any better. This one wasn't going to heal pretty. *Another scar for the memory bank, I guess...*

The nurse stood up straight. "Just wait here while I get the doctor to come in and take a final look at you, then we'll see about getting you discharged, okay?"

Taylor said nothing. The girl went to leave the room, nearly bumping into Calvin in the doorway as he breezed in. The door closed behind him, and Calvin tucked his phone in his pocket, a look of urgency on his face. He must have just been on the phone with Quantico. Since Taylor had been put out of commission, they sent for someone to pick Hans Stender up, and now he was being questioned there.

"Hey, how's the arm?" Calvin asked.

"Fine." Taylor sank into the hospital bed. Embarrassment burned her cheeks. This wasn't the first time Calvin was seeing her in this setting, all weak and pathetic. To distract from herself, she asked, "Were you on the phone with Quantico? What happened?"

There was a chair on the other side of the room, but Calvin just sat at the foot of the bed. "Yeah, I just talked to Winchester. Two things."

Taylor blinked at him, waiting for him to go on.

"The first is, the chess thing leaked to the press. People are speculating we have a serial killer."

Oh, God. That was exactly what they needed. The media making up their own theories and giving the killer exactly what he wanted—attention. Taylor cringed at the idea.

"Great," Taylor muttered.

"It gets worse," Calvin said. "Stender is being let go."

"What?" Taylor demanded. A flare of anger burned in her chest. "How? Why?"

Calvin let out a long sigh. "Airtight alibi. He wasn't even in town when the last two victims were killed—he actually just got back this morning, after we found Stoll's body. There's a paper trail of receipts proving he'd been on a trip to pick up some custom wood for his shop."

Damn it. Taylor went to cross her arms but winced at the pain from her wound. She sighed and allowed her pale arms to rest against the white sheets. It'd be days, maybe weeks, before this stopped bothering her, and she was just going to have to get used to the pain. It had been a lot worse when she'd been shot in the abdomen all those years ago.

At least this wound won't ruin my life years later… I hope.

"But it wasn't all a waste," Calvin said, and Taylor's eyes snapped to him. "They dug more into Stender's life and found out he's been laundering money through the chess biz and trafficking black market antiques. Explains why he wasn't so eager to sell us stuff when we went in, huh?"

"I guess not a total waste," Taylor said. She knew something was up with Hans Stender; he just seemed dirty. But unfortunately, their search for Margot and Liam's killer was no closer to completion. That unsettled her more than anything. At the rate the killer was escalating, another body could drop any day.

"But also," Calvin said, "the chess piece found on Liam Stoll isn't one of Stender's pieces. And as for the score sheets, well, he's not the only one who uses them. Turns out it's a printable PDF you can get online, so it's not exactly gonna be easy to pinpoint who else could have them."

Of course, Taylor thought bitterly. Their lives could never be that simple.

"So, we have nothing," Taylor said.

"Yep," Calvin agreed. "Jack shit."

Taylor sighed. All three leads they'd tracked down so far had led them straight into the dirt. She tried to picture who the killer might be and came up with a blank image—and that was when she realized that since the first body dropped, they hadn't actually spent any time brainstorming an actual profile.

"Scott," Taylor said, "I don't know how long I'm going to be stuck here. We might as well do something useful. If you're sticking around, that is."

"Of course I am, and I thought you'd say something like that," Calvin said. "You're always on the clock, aren't you?"

"Almost always." She offered him a small, but uncomfortable smile. "Let's work on a profile. You go first."

Sometimes, Taylor felt like she didn't give Calvin enough space to speak his own mind and give his own theories—she wanted him to feel like an equal, so she let him start them out.

He slapped his knees and said, "Well… let's think about where he actually left the bodies. We know he didn't kill them onsite. And I mean, those are pretty risky spots to carry bodies—extremely public. So either he's totally reckless, or he's smart, because he didn't leave a shred of evidence."

Taylor nodded in agreement. "No cameras around where either body was found. Not a drop of DNA. And the chess connection, too, suggests some degree of intellect."

"Agreed."

Shutting her eyes, Taylor worked off what they had. Intelligent. Most likely a chess player—or at least, interested in chess. A figure began to form through the shadows of her mind.

"But the motive…" Taylor trailed off. What was the motive? With seemingly no connection between victim one and victim two, Taylor failed to understand what the motive could be. Instead, she thought about the tokens left at each site:

First, a score sheet.

Then, an actual piece.

A thought popped into her head, and she blurted: "Scott, on the first victim, he left a blank score sheet. But on the second, a knight. Was the 'knight' his first move?"

Calvin's eyebrows pulled together as he considered it. "Holy shit… it could be."

"And that means the next victim will have—"

Taylor was cut off by someone storming into the room. She looked up, expecting to see the doctor—but she was met face to face with Ben.

Her stomach bottomed out. He was the last person she expected to see here. Ben's eyes flitted between Taylor and Calvin, still seated at the edge of her bed. His eyes shot Calvin daggers, as if silently sending a message—and Calvin seemed to get it, because he got up.

"We'll talk this through later, Sage," he said. "I'll be in the hall. See you out there."

Taylor weakly waved. "Thanks, Scott."

Calvin left, and the door closed Taylor in the room with Ben. A moment of silence stretched between them, and Taylor wished she could hide under the sheets, hide from this. More importantly, she wanted to know why he was here, because she hadn't requested that the hospital inform him.

"How did you—" Taylor began, but Ben cut her off.

"The nurse called me. I'm listed as your emergency contact. I'm your husband, remember?"

"Of course, but…" Taylor swallowed her nerves. With everything going on, Ben was honestly the last person she expected—or even wanted—to see. "Why did you come?" she asked.

Reluctantly, Ben approached the bed. "I needed to see if you're okay. Judging by the way you were sitting around chatting with your partner… it seems like you're fine."

"I'm sorry. I didn't think you would care," she said, which was true—so true that she hadn't even considered calling Ben under the automatic assumption that he wouldn't come.

"You're still my wife, Taylor." Ben sat on the edge of the bed, but he was even farther down from where Calvin had sat, and that only made Taylor's heart hurt more. Her own husband wouldn't even get as close to her as a coworker. That one stung. Awkwardly shifting his weight, Ben asked, "Do you need a ride home?"

"No. Scott went and grabbed my car—he drove it here for me." Since Taylor had met Calvin in D.C. earlier, she'd left her car in a parking lot while they'd driven Calvin's to Stender's place. After hurrying Taylor to the hospital after the Stender attack, Calvin had taken a cab to Taylor's car and driven it back, so it'd be waiting for her when she got out—as he already knew she wasn't willing to A) accept a ride home, and B) leave her car to be broken into in a random parking lot. Taylor appreciated that, and Calvin had been rock solid today—but Belasco's ominous warning still hung in the back of her mind.

"Right. Scott," Ben said bitterly. He stood up, wiping his hands on his pants. "Anyway… if you're fine, then, I should go."

Taylor's heart dropped at Ben's frosty tone. He drove all this way just to leave so quickly? What was even the point? It felt like he was rubbing salt in her wounds. Taylor couldn't resist her bitter remark.

"That's a long drive just to say hi and go. You could have just called the hospital and saved the gas money."

"What kind of husband would I be if I didn't at least check?" he said as he turned his back. Ben hesitated, and for a moment, Taylor hoped he would change his mind, turn around and at least give her a damn hug. But he just said, "See you at home."

With that, Ben was gone. The ice from his visit rested over the hospital room. Taylor's teeth practically chattered.

In all their years of marriage, Ben had never—*never*—acted this way. And alone in that hospital bed, Taylor could no longer escape facing the reality that this was a seismic shift in their marriage.

It may never recover. They may never be the same.

The word *divorce* spiraled in her mind.

***

Half an hour later, Taylor had been discharged from the hospital. Ever since Ben left, she had just been numb. She walked out of the hospital doors, into the damp, early September night, and breathed in deep. A chill ran through her bones.

Calvin walked out behind her. Even though he really didn't have to, he'd waited around to see her to her car. "Hey," he said, "you wanna grab a super-late dinner?"

Taylor turned to him, hugging herself, and forced a smile. She had wanted to get lunch with him earlier, but now, the idea of staying out more and socializing sounded exhausting. Her battery had officially run out, and besides, if there was any truth to Belasco's warning, the last thing she wanted was to face a potential betrayal from Calvin tonight. Her heart wouldn't be able to take it.

"Thanks, Scott, but I'm okay. I'm tired."

"Yeah, don't blame you." He half-smiled. "Guess I'll see you at work tomorrow?"

"Yeah, of course."

"Take care, Agent Sage." He gently patted her shoulder before he went into the parking lot to find his car. Taylor watched, relishing in the feeling of the late-summer air before she went to find her own vehicle.

Taylor didn't want to socialize anymore, it was true. But she also didn't want to go home to Ben. After the way he'd treated her earlier? Not a chance. Sleeping alone in a cold, empty hotel room also sounded like a recipe for disaster. Taylor pulled out her phone and checked the time. It was late—but she was a lot closer to Baltimore than she was to her home in Pelican Beach.

Tonight, she was staying with her parents.

CHAPTER FIFTEEN

With his hands firm on the steering wheel, the grandmaster drove his car through the starry night, his latest piece safe in the passenger seat of his car. He had given himself the name, because he knew no other title would fit—after all, no one knew chess better than him. Especially not the police. With their lazy response to his recent plays, he was starting to realize that, maybe, there wasn't anybody out there worthy of playing against him at all.

He already knew he was the best, after all. But above everything, what he craved was a challenge. Someone to see his talent and actually play back. So, he'd decided that he needed to go bigger. His last two moves were too dull, too simple.

But this next move would attract the attention of a worthy adversary. It had to.

The grandmaster smiled to himself and glanced at the seat next to him. "You know I'm going to make you famous, right?"

His latest piece was still fast asleep, unable to respond, but the grandmaster didn't care; he'd learn soon enough.

"It's just crazy to me," he said, "how those pigs haven't even made the connection yet. They haven't even started the game. Even though the world can see it now, the game we're playing."

He paused as he came up to a red light. It was four a.m. in D.C., and the streets were like a ghost town. But he liked the silence. He'd never had much of it in his life. In and out of the system, tossed between households of screaming children and adults who couldn't contain their rage, he had spent most of his life surrounded by too much noise. He hated it. That was why he thrived at the darkest hours of the night, when only the crickets could join him. *Silence.* He would give anything for it.

"It's their loss, really," he continued as the light turned green, and he drove forward. "I'm giving them the story of the century, and they're not even responding. But don't worry—I'm going to make sure they can't ignore you. You won't be put to waste." He glanced at his piece. Emotion welled up inside him at the beauty. "I won't waste you…"

In the passenger seat, his piece shifted. He'd probably wake soon, but the knock to the back of the head still had him out cold. That was okay—they'd arrive at their destination soon. He turned another street corner like a cunning snake through the night.

"Life is like a game of chess; did you know that?" he went on. "Some of us—like me—are meant to be grandmasters. Indispensable. Undefeatable. But others—like you—are more like pawns. Easily disposed of."

He paused, allowing himself to bask in the genius, the insightfulness of his words. The world couldn't see him the way he was meant to be seen, but that was okay; the grandmaster knew who he was. And whoever his opponent would be—they would know too.

Someday, the whole world would understand how great he was, and all those who had opposed him would pay. For his biggest game ever, he was going to win the ultimate prize: a lifetime of true pride.

"But that's not to say you have no use," he continued, addressing his piece. "Not at all. In fact, people like you are the most important, because you have a very crucial role to play in ensuring that people like me get to win. One could argue that is the greatest honor of all. Without you, dear bishop, there would be no me."

He pulled up to the alleyway and parked the car. Smiling to himself, he checked his reflection quickly in the mirror.

He looked like a god.

Satisfied with himself, he got out of the car and stepped into the cool night, stretching his limbs. Someday, someone else would drive him around, but for now, he was okay with being his own chauffer. No one else could be trusted with a job as important as this, and he had honor; he was no cheater. He had never accepted help from anybody.

He made his way to the passenger door and opened it, pulling his latest piece out by grabbing under his armpits. He dragged him toward the alleyway, deeper into the obscurity of the night.

"Almost there," he murmured.

Suddenly, his latest piece gasped for air—and his eyes popped open.

The grandmaster smiled. Looked like they'd have to finish early, after all.

This will get their attention.

CHAPTER SIXTEEN

Taylor poked at the cold plate of spaghetti in front of her. Across the table at her parents' house, her father, Randall, watched her silently—Taylor could feel him looking, but she'd been purposefully avoiding any real conversation since she got in the door. It wasn't that she didn't want to talk to her father; she just didn't want to explain why she was here, and not at home with Ben.

"You know I can heat that up, sweetheart," her dad said, nodding at the food.

Taylor glanced at him, then popped a cold noodle in her mouth. The tomatoey flavor, along with the cold temperature, brought her back to her childhood. She used to always eat leftover spaghetti late at night when she was studying for exams in high school. "You know I like it cold, Dad." She sighed and glanced out the kitchen window, where it was dark. "Besides, it's a little late to be eating. Sorry I showed up like this."

"It's fine," her dad said, rubbing his eye beneath his glasses, "but I'd really like to know why my daughter is here at ten p.m. instead of at home with her husband."

That had been his first question when she'd arrived, too. *"Where's Ben? Is everything okay?"*

No, everything was not okay. Taylor hadn't even told her own parents that she was infertile either. And she definitely didn't want to talk about it now. It wasn't exactly an easy topic to bring up. Taylor's parents had never put pressure on her to give them grandchildren, and she'd always appreciated that. However, she'd decide herself that kids were the path she wanted someday, and she knew her mom and dad were excited to be grandparents someday. More guilt sank Taylor's heart. This was exactly why she didn't want to talk about it.

"Yes, Dad, it's fine," she said. "We just needed a night apart. That's all."

Her dad lifted a gray, bushy brow. "You know I can read you like a book, Taylor. Things with you and Ben haven't been right for a while. At some point, you're gonna have to let your mother and I in."

Taylor's mom was sleeping upstairs—she'd always been an early riser, and her schedule reflected that. Bed by ten, up by six. Taylor was sort of grateful her mom wasn't up, though, because she wouldn't be able to let the Ben conversation go until she got an answer. Normally, Taylor's dad was more understanding, or at least less pushy, so she hoped she'd be able to talk him down. And there was no better way to distract him than to bring up a case.

"Dad, seriously," she said, "let's just drop it. I'm actually working a pretty major case right now."

That perked her dad's ears up. "Oh?"

Taylor ate another cold, stiff noodle. "Yeah. It's new, and I don't have much information yet… only two victims so far. But we think it may be a serial killer." She paused, her stomach sinking as she thought of the past two victims—and who might be next. "Dad, I'm afraid he might escalate."

"Well, he just might," he said, "and you'll have to face that when it happens. You're a good agent, so I know that if you had any solid leads, you wouldn't be here right now."

"I have nothing," she confessed, and it was true; Hans Stender had been a big, tall brick wall, and now Taylor was forced to sit here and eat while a killer was on the loose.

"Well, maybe I can help," her dad said. "Tell me what you *do* have."

As a clinical psychologist with an emphasis on serial killers, Taylor had always trusted her father's opinion. She came to him often when she was stumped on a case. In fact, if it hadn't been for her father, she never would have gotten to Jeremiah Swanson as fast as she did on the last case. It was right here in this kitchen that she'd finally cracked her last case. Maybe now, she'd have the same luck.

"Okay, well…," she ran over the details in her mind. "Our first victim was Margot Withers; we found her at the Capitol building. Maybe you saw her on the news—she accused that senator, Frank Petit, of sexual misconduct."

Her dad ran his hand over his stubble. "Yeah, the blonde girl. We heard about her death on the news. I didn't realize you were on the case. You think the senator did it?"

"Well, no. The senator she accused isn't even in the country, and with the second victim, there seems to be no connection to the political world at all. In fact, the second victim was a very normal, everyday type of guy. He didn't know Margot Withers. And he was left in a totally different setting. With a different—but seemingly related—token."

"Ah," her dad said. "We're dealing with tokens. That's not good."

"I know. They aren't just any tokens, either. On Margot, we found a chess score sheet. On the second victim, Liam, we found a chess piece—a knight. I'm sure you can see where I'm going with this."

Her dad nodded. "The killer has some sort of fascination with chess."

"Exactly. I can't help but feel like he's sending a message, but I haven't figured out what, exactly… first, a blank score sheet, then a first piece… it's almost like he was making a move."

"Almost like he's playing a game," her dad said, "and he wants you to play back."

Taylor's pulse quickened. Playing a game. That was what this whole thing had felt like. If the score sheet was blank, and the knight was the first move—then what did he expect them to do next?

Make *their own* move?

"But how can we?" Taylor wondered aloud. "I'd be open to baiting him to come out, but how can I do that without him hurting someone else?"

"You probably can't," her dad reasoned. "If this is a game to him, then each time he wants to play, he's going to kill another person. That would be my best guess, anyway. You only have two victims so far, so I can't say it with certainty… but I have a pretty strong feeling."

"So do I." Taylor grit her teeth. "But I don't want a third."

Resting his hands behind his head, her dad leaned back in the chair. "Well, let's take a step back for a second here. We have a killer who is making a first move, and he clearly wants you to make one back. But he hasn't set it up so you can make one back—that you can see, anyway." His gray eyes flashed. "There must be something you're not seeing here, sweetheart. Something you missed."

Taylor pondered this. Something missing; that seemed completely plausible. But what? They had thoroughly examined the crime scenes, and Taylor talked to forensics; there was no DNA, and the only significant things left were the tokens. Neither victim was killed at the scene, and there was nothing to suggest how the killer even got them to each location. By car seemed the most likely, but there were a million cars in this city.

"Anyway." Her dad stood up and scooped up Taylor's almost-finished plate—he knew she wouldn't be finishing it. "Why don't you worry about it all in the morning? You look like you need some serious rest."

He went and scraped her food off in the trash, and Taylor sluggishly stood up. She hadn't even realized how tired she was. This had been a long, exhausting day, but would sleeping really help? Last night's nightmare crept back into her mind. *Angie.*

"Maybe I could bounce a few more ideas off you?" Taylor asked timidly. She wasn't done thinking about the case.

Her dad sighed, hands on his hips. "You're exhausted, Taylor. I can see it all over you. Go get some sleep. This isn't healthy for your body. Or your mind. You're a better agent—and detective—when you're well-rested."

"But—" She took a deep breath. "But I had a nightmare the other night, and…"

That seemed to get his attention. His eyes glided over her, and for a moment, he looked more like a psychologist than her father. "What kind of nightmare?"

"It was about Angie."

Her dad's face dropped, the color draining from it. He shifted his weight. "Oh… well… you should still get some sleep."

Taylor could tell he didn't want to talk about it. Talking about Angie was never easy in their household, and Taylor herself didn't like to bring her up much. But that nightmare had been so real, so vivid, that she didn't want to go to bed and experience another like it. She'd rather stay awake and drive herself to insanity thinking about the case.

But that wasn't her father's burden; she couldn't put that on him, and so she resigned. "Okay, Dad. Thanks. Goodnight."

With that, Taylor went upstairs, into the guest room, where she had a stash of pajamas in the drawer. Her sister was still heavy on her mind.

Angie's disappearance had always been like a malignant growth to Taylor's family. Not an immediate death sentence, but more of a slow death, a heartbreak that never truly died. Taylor sat down on the edge of the bed as a sense of defeat weighed on her.

Suddenly, a knock at the door. It opened, and her mother stood in the doorway in a pair of floral silk pajamas.

"Mom!" Taylor said. She hadn't expected to see her. Her mother hurried into the room and gave her a hug, and Taylor breathed in her familiar smell, like lavender. Her mom was incredibly empathetic and intuitive—surely, she could sense Taylor's despair from a mile away. Not just about Angie, but about Ben.

"Hi, sweetie." Her mom sat next to her on the bed, smiling warmly.

"What are you doing awake?" Taylor asked.

"I heard you come in, and I swear, the whole mood in the house changed. I suddenly felt depressed!"

Taylor laughed. She had been spot-on in her prediction.

"Yeah, well… do I have to talk about it?" Taylor sulked.

Her mom patted her on the back lightly. "Sweetie, I won't force you to. But if you're here, I can only assume it means you're fighting with Ben."

That was one way to put it. Taylor loved her mother, but the last thing she wanted was to get her reaction to all the drama she'd created. Instead, she pivoted it back to what had been more recently pressing her mind: Angie. Taylor's mom had always been more open to discussing her than her father, which Taylor always thought was sort of funny as her dad was the psychologist and her mom was the artist. Weren't psychologists supposed to talk it out, while artists kept it all in and painted away their feelings?

"I'd rather not talk about Ben, honestly," Taylor said. "But… there was something else. I've been thinking about Angie a lot lately."

Her mom's brows pinched, and she began rubbing Taylor's back at a slower pace. "Oh, honey… I think about her every day."

"I know." Taylor swallowed, choked up. "I do too, Mom, but…" She sighed heavily. "I know she's gone. But sometimes I still hold onto hope that something will turn up, and we'll find her again, you know?"

Silence hung in the air, and Taylor worried that she'd said too much and was going to upset her mother. But she kept rubbing her back in those soothing, circular motions. Finally, she said, "We may never know, sweetheart. I try not to think about the future, in this case. Instead, I remember the past. Even though Angie is gone now, we still have the memories of her from when she was little. Those memories are real, you know. It's okay to think about them, even if they hurt."

Taylor considered her mother's words. It was true—Taylor had spent a lot of time suppressing her memories of Angie. Maybe that was why the dreams had come out. It was Angie's way of clawing out from her subconscious. But that didn't explain why they had suddenly started now, two decades later. Taylor had never had such vivid dreams of her before.

"I know, Mom," Taylor said. "Thanks."

Her mother smiled. "Do you want to know my favorite memory of you two?"

Taylor nodded.

Still with those wistful eyes, her mom said, "You were about six years old, and Angie was eight. Eight is such a bratty age, you know that? Six is much more curious… but Angie was at the age where she was starting to feel a little jealous when you got the attention."

Taylor grinned as she remembered her sister when they were little. "Mom, she was always like that."

It was true. When Taylor was born, Angie was no longer the baby, and she'd lashed out a few times… but ultimately, her childish jealousy was never stronger than her love for her. Sure, there had been some moments of envy, but in the end, Taylor had more memories of Angie tucking her into bed and sharing her toys with her.

"Yes, she certainly could be." Her mom chuckled warmly. "But this time was really bad. I was trying to get you two to work as a team and bake some cookies, but Angie wanted to control everything. She wouldn't let little Taylor even add sprinkles! I was so mad at her."

Taylor searched her mind for this memory. It took a moment for her to unearth it. She hadn't thought of this in years—it was like greeting an old, forgotten friend. But she remembered making the cookies. She remembered the sprinkles, and Angie being such a brat about them.

Her mom continued, "I eventually told Angie that by not allowing you to put the sprinkles on, she was preventing you from learning an essential skill in life. I told her that if you didn't learn now, you may never be able to sprinkle cookies…"

"Mom!" Taylor laughed and playfully smacked her arm. "That's so manipulative," she said jokingly.

"Oh, I know. It was awful." Her mom laughed. "But it turned Angie right around. Suddenly, she wanted to be the best sprinkle mentor for you she could be. What a sweet girl."

More silence befell them, but it was nostalgic. A deep longing tugged at Taylor's heart. It had been so long since she'd had a sister, she'd almost entirely forgotten what it was like.

"I wish she were still here," she said absentmindedly. "I wish I still had a sister."

"You've always had a sister," her mom said. "Always. Just because she left, doesn't mean you're an only child."

Taylor had never thought about it like that. It was true, she'd spent most of her life as an only child now, and those memories of Angie were so distant, sometimes it felt like they weren't even real.

But they *were* real.

Her mom was right; Taylor did have a sister. She was born with one. And even if she'd live the rest of her life never knowing what happened to Angie, that didn't mean Angie was never here.

Overwhelmed with emotion, she went in for a hug. Teary-eyed, her mom laughed and patted her on the back.

"It's not like you to be so emotional, sweetie," her mom said, "but I love it. Thank you."

"Thanks, Mom." Taylor pulled away. "I really needed this."

***

After washing her face and brushing her teeth in her parents' familiar, comforting bathroom, Taylor went to bed and got under the covers, fully expecting to stare at the ceiling all night. Even after the comforting conversation with her mom, her mind was on high alert. Because after her mom had gone to bed, Taylor was left alone with her thoughts again.

But before she knew it, her eyelids were heavy, and as much as she tried to keep them open, she couldn't fight it. Taylor descended into a deep, dark sleep.

At first, she was comforted by the stillness. Everything was quiet and flowing. She was safe. Safe with her parents, away from Ben, away from work. Things were okay again; Angie was gone, but it was like her mom said—that didn't mean she was never here. Taylor took comfort in this darkness. In her delusional state, she even felt happy.

But then, a voice:

"Taylor."

It was Angie. Again.

Taylor opened her eyes to a wide field under a starry sky. The full moon bled down on her. Partially aware she was dreaming, Taylor said to herself, *You'll wake up soon. Don't worry.*

But Angie spoke again:

"You have to find me. If you don't, I'll die, and it will be all your fault."

"No!" Taylor shouted. She spun around, her heart thundering in her chest. But the field around her was endless. Angie's voice bellowed, seemingly from the sky.

"If you can't find me, I'll die," she sang again. "It will be all your fault."

"I'm looking!" Taylor cried. A surge of emotions ran through her—guilt, fear, desperation. She had to find Angie. She could make this right. She ran and ran, but the field extended on forever. The sky was bigger than she had ever seen it. It dwarfed her, and each star grew brighter and brighter the farther she ran.

Something heavy landed behind her, shaking the entire earth. Taylor spun around, only to be met by a massive black wall. She looked up, and up, until she realized—

No, it wasn't a wall.

It was a massive chess piece. A knight. It reached into the night sky, tall and sinister, surrounded by those too-bright stars.

"It will be all your fault," the voice said again, but this time, it was distorted; it wasn't Angie's.

"Where are you?" Taylor shouted anyway. "Where are you?"

The ground began to vibrate. Taylor struggled to hold herself up. Panic flew through her chest, and she tried to catch herself—but she fell to her knees, falling right through the earth, into a black pit.

"Where are you?" she repeated, over and over again. Her own voice spiraled around her head.

Everything rattled around her, like she was experiencing an earthquake. The whole world trembled, and the tremendous sound of mountains breaking and oceans overflowing filled her ears.

Her eyes popped open to a stucco ceiling.

While her body was completely still, a rattling sound still shook something nearby, but Taylor couldn't focus on it. The dream still lingered, heavy on her mind.

That had been the most real yet.

Soaked in sweat, Taylor sat up in her parents' guest room bed, feeling like she'd been hit by a train. As reality returned to her, she cursed herself for falling asleep. She knew this was going to happen. The feeling of the dream still resonated through her, and her heart pounded loudly against the wall of her chest.

Also, the phone beside her was ringing.

"Damn it," she muttered. Panicked, she went to answer it.

Unsurprisingly, it was Calvin Scott.

"Scott," she answered, catching her breath, "tell me you have good news."

"Afraid not, Sage," he said. "Where are you? I'll come pick you up." He paused; Taylor knew what was coming next. "We have another body."

Taylor fell back into her own sweaty sheets and heaved out a sigh. *When will it end?*

CHAPTER SEVENTEEN

With Calvin at her side, Taylor walked up to the building they'd been called to, where police swarmed the area. It was a strip on the west side of D.C., and the cleanliness of the streets spoke of wealth in the neighborhood. It was barely six a.m., and the sun was peeking over the buildings, creating long shadows over the streets. A chill ran through the air, raising the goosebumps on Taylor's arms beneath her jacket.

In truth, when Calvin called her this morning, it hadn't exactly caught Taylor off guard. In her gut, she had felt another body was about to drop, but now that it had actually happened, her anxiety was on high alert. She hated that she hadn't solved the case yet, but what was she supposed to do? They had nothing. She just prayed this crime scene would, at the very least, point to the killer.

It all made Taylor wonder who they were about to discover in this back alley.

The police had caution taped off the alleyway beside a building with a sign that read C-2-IT. After hearing where the body was discovered—in the alleyway behind the business—Taylor had done some quick recon, and she learned that C-2-IT was a staffing agency that provided maids, babysitters, dog walkers, and other services to wealthy clients. Liam Stoll had been found at a travel agency, which was somewhat similar, only in the sense that it was an agency. But the US Capitol had nothing to do with either place, so Taylor failed to see the connection.

After showing their badges to the officers standing guard, Taylor and Calvin slipped over the caution tape, stepping into the dark, shadowed, and cold back alleyway. Even back here was clean—there was a single dumpster, but no rotting garbage smell or trash on the ground.

Up ahead, more officers stood guard. As they drew closer, Taylor started to make out the scene beneath the obscurity of the shadows.

And what she saw sent a grisly chill up her spine.

There was blood. *Everywhere.*

Swallowing a massive portion of the concrete ground, the lake of blood extended so far that it pooled into the edges of the buildings on each side. And in the middle of that blood was the body of a young man, his clothes drenched in his own gore.

Taylor's throat tightened into a straw. Air could barely reach her lungs.

She'd expected to find a scene similar to the last two, with a body lying there, no blood. But this was so much worse. She instinctively covered her mouth as bile churned in her gut.

Calvin must have noticed because he asked, "Sage, you good?"

Gathering herself, Taylor nodded. She generally didn't lose face like this on the job, but after the no sleep and the nightmares and the anxiety, this type of gore was the last thing she wanted to see. She needed to keep herself together. So far, this case had been a poor performance for her, on an emotional level. She made a mental note not to let her personal life affect her work life; that had always been her motto.

"I'm okay," she said, although she was shaky. "Let's take a closer look."

A young officer, who had been taking photos of the scene, backed off with a nod when Taylor and Calvin approached. "Do we have an ID on the victim?" Taylor asked the cop.

She nodded grimly. "His name is Michael West. He's a schoolteacher."

Another good Samaritan, presumably. Anger gnawed at Taylor. "Thank you," she said, dismissing the other officer. "We'll take it from here."

She faced the body. This was ugly, but she needed to get in there and see what she could unearth. Sliding on a black glove, Taylor had to step between streams of blood to avoid getting her shoes in it and get closer to the body. Calvin hung back and watched. Carefully, Taylor crouched down and examined the body. The manner of stabbing appeared to be the same—a single, clean wound to the chest, with minimal damage to the clothing.

But the pure carnage of this was vastly different from the previous two. So what did it mean? The killer was stepping up—but why? He was becoming more brazen, more confident… or just messier. Or maybe it was frustration. She thought about what her dad said last night, about how the killer wanted them to "make a move."

Was he frustrated that they hadn't done so yet?

Could this be the retaliation?

More importantly—was this even the same killer? With such a starkly different scene, Taylor had to be sure. They had been called specifically because the officers on site associated the single stab wound with the case, which was alerted to Winchester. But until Taylor saw a chess connection, she wouldn't be convinced this was done by the same guy.

She glanced down the body. The victim was wearing a white shirt that was now almost entirely blood red. And he wore black slacks. This was probably what he wore in general when he taught at his school. Not only that, but there was a silver cross around his neck. *A religious man?*

As she looked for more details, she stopped at the pocket of his pants. Something stood out.

An unusual, oblong shape poked out beneath it, similar to what she'd found on Liam Stoll.

Pulse pounding, Taylor carefully used her gloved hand to peer into the pocket.

A single chess piece—a bishop—was tucked into the pocket of the victim's pants.

Taylor's breath caught in her throat as she carefully removed it. Her dream crept back into her mind—the massive chess piece. It all felt eerily related, like she was still dreaming now.

"What'd you find, Sage?" Calvin asked, and Taylor snapped out of her daze.

She faced him with the chess piece in hand. When Calvin saw it, his brows shot up.

"Holy shit. It's him," he said.

Taylor stepped away from the body. She removed an evidence bag from her pocket and carefully dropped the chess piece in.

"But it doesn't make sense," Calvin said. "This scene is way different than the last two. This guy was clearly murdered here. Why switch it up?"

"I don't know," Taylor said absentmindedly, still stuck on the chess piece, observing it in the bag. On the bottom was a specific marker—a tiny white V. The same as the other piece.

"Maybe it's not even him," Calvin reasoned. "I mean… the chess thing *did* just leak to the press. It was all over the local news last night. It could be a copycat. People move fast in this city."

A copycat didn't seem likely to Taylor. Still stuck on that white V, she pulled out her phone and looked at the evidence photos from Liam Stoll's murder. In it were pictures of the previous chess piece from all angles. Taylor remembered the white V from before, but she needed to see them together for herself again.

They were an exact match.

"Scott, they're from the same set," Taylor said. "A copycat is too unlikely. This is him. But he's escalating, and he's doing it fast."

"No kidding," Calvin said. "Okay, a copycat is out the window. So why'd he switch up his MO?"

That was the question. Taylor didn't have much to go off yet, but she decided to share what she'd discussed with her father last night—maybe Calvin would have some insight.

"I was talking to my father last night," she told him. "He's a clinical psychologist, so I've always trusted his advice. He's helped me out on a lot of cases throughout my career."

She paused, realizing she'd gotten overly personal. Calvin watched her intently. Maybe awestruck she was opening up about something that had to do with her actual *life*.

"Anyway," Taylor mumbled, "he threw around the idea that the killer is trying to play a game with us. That he wants us to make a move back."

"But how can we do that?" Calvin asked. "He's gotta know the FBI aren't about to kill somebody and leave them on the street with a chess piece in their pocket."

"That's the question, isn't it?" Taylor looked back at Michael West's body. At his glazed over eyes, staring up at the early morning sky. "What does he want us to do?"

Shutting her eyes, Taylor envisioned the killer. She had pictured him as very calculated before, very deliberate—and while she still felt that way, this new crime scene revealed a darker, more sinister side of the man. A deranged madman who left another human being to bleed out in a back alley.

Whatever move he wanted her to make, Taylor wasn't sure. But maybe learning more about the victim could give them another clue. Time to do some recon.

***

Half an hour later, Taylor and Calvin were in his car, parked at the side of the road with Taylor in the passenger seat. They'd come up with no solid leads based on the crime scene, and so now it was time to see what else they could learn about the victim. But Taylor had just gotten off the phone with their housekeeper, who confirmed that Michael West's wife was out of town. She had received news of her husband's death and was flying in, but until she landed, there was no way the FBI could question her.

Taylor's laptop was open on her lap as she dug into Michael's file. There wasn't much on him—his picture showed a mild-looking man with blue eyes and a gentle smile. Nothing like the corpse Taylor had just examined. Michael had never been arrested—by all manner of speaking, he seemed like an honest, hard-working, religious man with a pleasant life.

So what led him to that alley?

Taylor could feel Calvin staring at her in her periphery. She glanced at him and asked, "What are you thinking, Scott? Any new ideas?"

"Nah." He adjusted himself in the seat, fixing his jacket blazer. "Actually, I was wondering—why the hell did I pick you up in Baltimore? I thought you'd be back in Pelican Beach."

Taylor stiffened. This was going to get personal fast, and discomfort moved through her. She didn't need to tell her partner about her relationship issues. Besides, now wasn't the time.

But he was going to ask anyway, apparently, because he said, "Everything okay at home?"

Swallowing the knot in her throat, Taylor shrugged. "It's fine, Scott. We should focus on the case."

"I know you hate when I ask about this stuff," Calvin said. "I got a vibe from your husband the other day, though. And you were pretty hurt, so I figured you would've gone home to be with him. Why'd you stay with your parents?"

Taylor tried not to be annoyed, but it was hard when this felt so personal. At the same time, she didn't want to make things hostile with Calvin, so she decided to give him some breadcrumbs. "We've been fighting," she said. "I'd rather not get into it."

"I get it," he said. "Well, I'm here if you need anything."

Taylor looked at him, and he offered her a half-smile. She appreciated the gesture, although Belasco's warning crept back into her head as she stared at her partner. Whatever betrayal she'd predicted had shown no signs of starting. Although she was annoyed that he was asking personal questions when they had a serious lead to chase down.

Forcing a smile back, Taylor said, "Thanks, Scott. Now… the case? It's kind of important."

"Right, sorry. I'll drop it. Refocusing." He paused, thinking. "So, the wife isn't an option. Who else would know this guy best? That officer said he was a schoolteacher, so he must be pretty known in his community. Maybe he has some friends we can talk to."

Looking down his profile, Taylor saw that he worked at St. Paul's Catholic School. She pulled out her phone and did a quick search on the GPS and found it was just barely across town, not far from where Michael lived. They could make it within twenty minutes, while the school was just opening up.

"Not just any school—a Catholic school," Taylor said. She closed her laptop and did up her seat belt. "Should we pay them a visit?"

CHAPTER EIGHTEEN

The high walls of St. Paul's Catholic School towered all around Taylor as she and Calvin entered, their footsteps echoing off the tiled floors. It had been a long time since Taylor had stepped foot in a high school—considering she was thirty-four, and graduated at eighteen, she never had much of a reason to go back, aside from the odd interview for a few different cases back when she used to live in Portland.

Being in a school didn't exactly help her to forget her nightmare about Angie, either, considering the last time Taylor actually *had* a sister was in high school. Fleeting memories of seeing Angie in the halls and in the cafeteria, being a normal teenage girl, flared in her mind. It was a grim thought to know she'd always know her older sister by her younger self, and never get to see her become a grown woman.

Who would she be now if she hadn't gone missing? Would she be able to help Taylor through this awful situation with Ben? Would Angie have her own partner?

Taylor tried to shake those thoughts away; now wasn't the time. Besides, this school was a far cry from the one they'd attended, which was more generic and typically American, while this school had a prestigious authority about it. The halls were mostly quiet, as classes hadn't started yet, but Taylor and Calvin passed by a few girls in pine green uniforms at their lockers, who politely nodded at the agents as they passed. More students would trickle in soon, so Taylor would rather get this over with quick before causing a scene. There was nothing high schoolers loved more than gossip.

The news of Michael West's death wouldn't have reached the student body yet, although Taylor had called ahead to inform the headmaster of what happened, and that they would be visiting. He had told them his office was on the second floor, and that he'd be waiting. Taylor and Calvin made their way through the clean halls until they found a large, mahogany door that said HEADMASTER LEWIS on it.

Taylor knocked, and after a moment, a short, pudgy man with a jolly face opened the door. He had big freckles on his balding head and near white hair, but he gave off a jovial aura. Despite this, the look on his face was solemn; he was one of the few who knew about Michael

West's death, after all. And he would likely be the one to deliver the news to the student body.

"Hello," he said, "please, come in."

Obliging, Taylor and Calvin entered the office, which had a large wooden desk and was surrounded by bookshelves of literature—and bibles. A poster hung on the wall with the cross on it, and the office smelled of paper and cough drops.

"Have a seat, please," Headmaster Lewis said, gesturing to the two chairs in front of his desk as he scrambled to sit in his. Once everyone was seated, Lewis sighed. "I am *so* sorry to hear about Michael. His wife must be devastated."

"Thank you for meeting with us so quickly," Taylor said. "We haven't been able to speak to Mr. West's wife, yet, but she has been notified."

"Well, it's just awful," Lewis said. "Michael was an upstanding teacher. His students are going to be heartbroken. It's so sad, too—he was one of our newest, yet most beloved staff.

"We're sorry for your loss," Calvin cut in.

Taylor nodded in agreement. "Yes, and we'll make this quick so you can take time to prepare to tell them what happened." She cleared her throat and folded her hands on her lap. "Now, can you tell us if Michael had any enemies? Anyone who might want to hurt him?"

"Oh, heavens, no!" Lewis nearly chuckled. "Michael was adored. I don't think you understand how much people loved him. Sometimes the students can be a bit short with me, or with the other staff, which is perfectly natural for their age. But Michael was beloved across all grades, and among the faculty, as well. No—there isn't a soul on this earth I know of who might want to hurt a man like him."

Of course, Taylor thought. The chances of the killer being anywhere near the victim's world seemed unlikely, considering the first two victims were unconnected to each other. They would dig into a connection between them and Michael West, but Taylor was pretty confident they'd find nothing.

"You mentioned he was a new staff member," Taylor said. "How long had he been working here? Classes just started, but you said everyone loved him, so he must have been here before the summer."

"The latter half of last year," he said. "He filled in for a teacher on maternity leave."

Taylor nodded. This was all good information. But one thing about Michael's crime scene seemed most important:

"And do you think a 'bishop' has anything to do with Michael?" Taylor asked.

Lewis shrugged. "We didn't get to know him too well personally. I think maybe he was a priest before he became a teacher. Or maybe it was a bishop? I'm not too sure, unfortunately."

Taylor needed to know more about Michael, and if she couldn't look at his house, she wanted the next best thing. Maybe that would provide more proof of the "bishop" connection.

"Headmaster Lewis, can we please take a look at Michael's desk before classes start?"

"Of course!" Lewis stood up. "Follow me—it's on the first floor."

***

Taylor yanked open the final drawer on Michael West's desk in his classroom. Like the others, it contained nothing but a neat stack of folders, some that held graded tests, others files on students.

Nothing hinted at any connection between him and the last two victims. Nor him and the killer—or chess and bishops, for that matter.

Frustrated, Taylor closed the drawer and glanced over the surface of Michael's neatly organized desk. A photo of him and his wife, smiling, made her heart hurt.

Calvin was across the room, glancing through the bookshelf, when Taylor walked over to him. When he looked at her, he didn't seem surprised as he asked, "Nothing?"

Taylor sighed in exhausted. "Nothing."

"Okay," Calvin breathed out. "What's next?"

Taylor glanced around the room, filled with desks and posters of scripture on the wall. Headmaster Lewis hadn't exactly pointed them to anything concrete, but this was a big school—Michael had many coworkers. Taylor checked the time—there was still about twenty minutes before classes would officially start. She could still reach some of his coworkers before they went to their rooms.

"Let's try the teacher's lounge," she suggested.

The hallways were busier now, and more uniformed students glanced at Taylor and Calvin, whispering to each other in gossip as they passed. Taylor kept her posture strong, her mind focused—she couldn't let all the eyes on her be a distraction. With the way this killer was escalating, it wouldn't be long before another body dropped. They needed to find him. And they couldn't afford to waste another second.

They located the teacher's lounge and knocked. A timid woman's voice said, "Hello, come in?"

Pushing the door open, Taylor and Calvin entered the teacher's lounge, greeted by the smell of coffee. There were only three teachers present—a short, plump woman, a young man who looked to be a substitute, and a hunched old man who must have been pushing seventy. They each held mugs of coffee as they stood around, rather than taking the couches. The concerned looks on their faces told Taylor they had heard the news. And they knew why she and her partner were here.

"Um, hi," Taylor said, feeling suddenly awkward. This was clearly an intimate moment between the staff, but she planned to make this quick.

"Are you the FBI agents here about Michael?" the woman asked.

Taylor nodded, glancing at Calvin.

"We were hoping to ask you a few questions really quick," Calvin said.

"Of course," the woman mumbled. The other two shifted on their feet, uncomfortable.

Taylor cleared her throat. "You all must have worked quite closely with Mr. West. Can you tell us anything about him that might be of significance? Any enemies he may have had? Or issues at home? Anything at all will help us in the investigation." She could feel the desperation come out in her voice and tried to regain composure.

"Not at all," the older man said. "Everyone loved Michael."

The others nodded in agreement.

"So, he had no enemies," Taylor said. "What about interests? Hobbies?"

"He loved scrapbooking with his wife," the woman chimed in. "And bake sales. They *loved* bake sales. They were a real church couple, honestly. This is just awful…"

A church-going man... a good Samaritan with no enemies…

None of this alluded at all to why he was picked as the victim. The other two had a purpose—the pawn and the knight. But what "role" would a teacher play in chess? Her only clue was the bishop chess piece, but a teacher wasn't the same as a bishop—even if he did work at a Catholic school. Frustration burned through her. It looked like no one at Michael's work was going to point them in the right direction.

Feeling worn down, Taylor thanked the teachers for their time, and she and Calvin returned to the hallway. Once alone, Calvin said, "I don't suppose 'scrapbooking' gave you any genius ideas about where to go next?"

Taylor sighed. "No. We're at another dead end."

"But there has to be a reason why this guy was picked," Calvin said. "Right?"

"There must be, but I don't think we'll find it here," she admitted. And if they couldn't speak to his wife, there was another option to dig up his past—and that would be through the internet. Taylor told Calvin, "Let's head back to HQ and see what we can find online."

***

Back at the briefing room at Quantico, Taylor clicked through pictures from Michael West's Facebook profile on her laptop. Each photo showed nothing but a picture-perfect life; his marriage to his wife, Becky, was all smiles. They looked like the type of couple who, if given the chance, would have had three kids and a big house with a golden retriever and white picket fence. A real American dream.

The dream Ben had for him and Taylor.

Taylor tried to shove that thought down as Calvin came back with two black coffees and handed one to her. She accepted it gratefully as he took the seat next to her. Stocking up on caffeine sounded like a good idea—especially after last night's nightmare. Maybe it would be better to induce insomnia to avoid another one of those damn dreams. She bitterly sipped on the hot drink as she focused back on her screen.

"Anything?" Calvin asked.

"Nothing significant," Taylor said. "Same as at the school—he's a happy guy who everyone loved. He doesn't seem to have any significant hobbies."

Taylor clicked on another photo of him and Becky. If Michael's profile didn't give anything away, maybe his wife's profile would. Taylor clicked on it and began scrolling. Becky West didn't have many public posts, mostly just photos of herself and Michael or pictures of animals like bunnies and cats.

But just as Taylor was thinking this was a lost cause, one of Becky's posts caught her eye. It was posted on February 14th last year, Valentine's Day. It showed a picture of Becky and Michael in each other's arms, standing on a grassy hill beneath a cerulean sky. The caption read:

Five years ago today, I didn't know my life would change forever.

I didn't know I'd meet you, Michael West, but I did. I was a nun, and as we all know, I was not allowed to wed...

But with you, I made a new commitment to God.

I left the convent, where you were also a bishop.

Two years later, we took an oath before God, and he gave us his blessing.

Now, we show our faith together.

Love you always, my bishop!!!

Taylor's heart raced as she read the post. Beside her, Calvin said, "Holy shit. He *was* a bishop."

"That's it," Taylor said. "That's the connection."

But of course it was—Michael West had a bishop piece in his pocket. This was the proof she needed. This was the connection.

And yet—she still didn't know what any of it meant.

A pawn, a knight, and a bishop...

She thought back to the conversation with her father. How he'd suggested that the killer wanted them to play back, but Taylor had no idea how to do that—and so her father suggested that she might be missing something.

Could it be a code?

Taylor's mind raced over the details of the case. Clearly, there was a code here, but she wasn't a master in the art of cracking them. Maybe it was time to bring in some outside help. Winchester was an option—but then again, Taylor had heard wind of a cryptographer who was temporarily working at HQ.

Maybe he'd be able to see what she was missing.

CHAPTER NINETEEN

As Taylor and Calvin approached the cryptographer's office in Quantico, she wasn't sure what she was expecting—she'd never met with him, after all, but she had heard fleeting stories around headquarters about how the man was a genius who could crack any code. He'd been working with the FBI for a decade and had helped break even the most convoluted codes left by serial killers. He was a huge asset to the bureau.

However, because of that, he wasn't always in town—sometimes he'd be stationed in other parts of the country and had apparently even worked with the CIA before. This was all according to Calvin, who had shared with her what he knew on the short walk they'd made from the briefing room to the cryptographer's office.

They entered the room. Inside, the lights were dim. They followed a short, but narrow hall into the main room, where an overhead projector illuminated the white brick walls with a magnified image of what appeared to be a hand-written note. A man, mid-forties, was hunched beside the projector, but he turned when Taylor and Calvin entered.

"Ah, hello there!" He shut off the projector, momentarily leaving the room pitch black before he flicked on the light. Taylor squinted as her eyes adjusted to the now fluorescent lighting.

The man wore a beige button-up and had glasses with thinning hair, but he also had a kind, dimpled smile and intelligent eyes. He extended a hand to Taylor first and shook it firmly, then Calvin.

"Agents, I heard you were coming," he said. "I'm Eric Lee, cryptography, but I guess you know that."

"Hi, Eric," Taylor said. "Thanks for meeting with us."

"I heard you might have a code to crack. Have a seat." He gestured to the table in the small room. Taylor and Calvin sat on one side, Eric on the other. He crossed his fingers and leaned forward. "So, what can I do for you?"

Where to even begin? Taylor thought. She decided to start with a simple overview: "Well," she began, "we have three bodies so far, each with a token relating to chess."

"Chess?" Eric's eyebrows went up, and interest sparked in his eyes. "Go on."

Taylor had brought her file, so she took out printed images of each murder and the tokens along with them. She laid them on the table and slid them toward Eric. He took in each one. There was:

Margot Withers, a blank chess sheet.

Liam Stoll, a knight.

Michael West, a bishop.

Eric nodded as he glanced over the images. "Okay, tell me what I'm seeing here."

Taylor pointed to Margot. "This victim was described as a 'pawn.' She was left with this blank chess sheet here. Our next victim did fencing for fun, so he is the 'knight,' as was confirmed by the piece in his pocket. The third previously worked as a bishop, therefore, he's our 'bishop.' As you can see…," Taylor paused and glanced at Eric. "We have a pattern emerging here."

"A game, if you will," Eric said, sounding mildly amused.

"Exactly," Calvin chimed in. "Special Agent Sage and I have a theory: he wants us to 'play.'"

"But we can't figure out how we're supposed to make a move," Taylor said. "And so I'm thinking there's something here that we're just not seeing."

"I guess that's where I come in," Eric said. "Okay. A pawn, a knight, and a bishop. It seems obvious these are his moves. But…," he looked closer at the photos. "I'm also not seeing what he could be telling you beyond that. Pawn, knight, bishop…," he muttered under his breath.

Taylor looked at the photos again too, trying to recall every detail she'd learned about the victims since their deaths. By all appearances, the three, as individuals, had nothing in common. Maybe it was best to divert away from trying to find a connection between them. But if not the victims themselves, then what other connection could it be? Could the places where the bodies were laid play any significance? Surely, they weren't random—the Capitol, a travel agency, and a staffing agency had little in common…

The thought hit her like a shovel over the back of the head.

They had their chess pieces—but what about the board?

"The locations," Taylor blurted. "Could they be a hint?"

"Potentially," Eric mused as he stroked his clean-shaven chin. "Can you tell me more about where they were found?"

Taylor grabbed each photo of the crime scene and snagged the marker that was on the table. In big, black letters, she wrote down the location of each murder:

US CAPITOL BUILDING: UNDERGROUND PARKING LOT.

TRAVEL AGENCY: "BEFORE YOU GO."

STAFFING AGENCY: "C-2-IT."

Taylor slid them back over to Eric, hoping he'd see something she didn't. Underground parking lot. *Before You Go. C-2-IT...* oddly enough, those stood out more than the Capitol.

"Okay, so we have three locations," Eric said. He intertwined his fingers beneath his chin and shut his eyes. Taylor watched in awe. Cryptographers fascinated her—she had always wanted to get more into it herself, and let this case be a reminder that she should get around to doing that.

Eventually, Eric seemed to have his idea, because he said, "In chess, they number and letter the boards. So, the 'before' in Before You Go—could that be B4? And C-2-IT—could it be C2?"

Excitement surged through Taylor. She hadn't thought about the numbers or letters on the board—Eric could be onto something.

"But hmm, that doesn't explain the Capitol," Eric said.

Taylor tried to get her mind in order, to think about what else it could all mean—but the realization hit her like a ton of bricks. She flipped open her file and went to the section about Margot's death.

She hadn't just been found in an underground parking lot—she'd been found in section A3.

"The first victim was in section A3," she told Eric.

They locked eyes, and it was like they were realizing it at the exact same time. Recognition darted across Eric's face, and Taylor said out loud:

"A3. B4. C2."

"Holy shit," Calvin said.

"That's it!" Eric exclaimed.

With a crazed look, he met Taylor's gaze; she must have looked equally as eager. This was a huge break—the first moment in this whole case when she actually felt like she'd *cracked* something.

"He's literally playing chess with us," Taylor said.

A smile curled at Eric's lips. "And he wants you to play back."

Taylor couldn't help but think he was getting some sort of enjoyment out of this—but in a way, she understood. Cracking a code was what fascinated him. Taylor would be lying if she said digging into the psyche of a serial killer didn't intrigue her as much as it disturbed her, and this was a huge piece of information.

Eric got up and grabbed a blank sheet of lined paper off a notebook on the nearby shelf and hurried back over. With the marker, he quickly made a chess board and labeled around the perimeter each corresponding letter and number.

On A3, he drew a pawn.

On B4, a knight.

On C2, a bishop.

"This is the code," Eric said, eyes bulging. "It's a series of plays."

Taylor's mouth went dry. She glanced at Calvin for his input—he'd been quiet, leaning back in the chair with his arms crossed, brows stitched like he was deep in thought. He leaned forward and placed his elbows on the table, hands wrung together.

"Okay, so these are his current moves," he said. "Which means if we can figure out his next move…"

"Then we can predict where the next kill will be," Taylor finished for him.

Her heart thumped loudly in her chest. If she could only predict where the next body would drop and also prevent the next victim from ever dying—that would be huge. Game changing. She'd not only save a life but save countless more from dying and stop a deranged madman from his clear path of escalation.

Okay, calm down, Sage, she told herself. First, they needed to figure out where the next move could be, so she needed to get back into the briefing room so she could think clearly.

Taylor stood, Calvin following. "Thanks, Eric," she said. "You've been a huge help." She snagged the paper with the chess board on it and left.

"You did all the work!" Eric exclaimed as Taylor sped out of the room, Calvin on her tail.

They made it back to the briefing room in only a couple short minutes—HQ was huge, but Taylor had practically run there. Hurrying back to the table, Taylor pulled out her laptop as Calvin sat next to her. Her fingers clacked against the keyboard as she typed in the three moves the killer had already done, figuring this could be some sort of play. And sure enough, it showed up right at the top:

THE VOLKOV MANEUVER.

A3, B4, C2…

And the next move was D4.

D4, D4… Taylor's mind raced. Why did that sound so familiar? She racked her brain for any clues. The last couple days flashed through her mind.

Then it hit her:

Dupont Circle. Where the chess tournament had been held.

The park was called Four Acres.

Taylor's heart leapt, and she practically shoved the table away as she stood. "Scott, we need to go now." She met his widened eyes. "I think I know where he'll strike next."

CHAPTER TWENTY

Taylor had her back pressed against the side of a building, hand on the gun holstered to her belt. It was nighttime, and darkness bathed D.C.'s streets. Calvin was right beside Taylor, but they were both so quiet that she could hear his breaths and the cars driving in the distance.

But Dupont Circle—more specifically, across from Four Acres Park—was eerily quiet at nearly three in the morning. In the dead of night, no one would see the two agents—or the entire SWAT team they had lurking in the shadows around the area.

After theorizing about the killer's potential next move, Taylor was convinced that D4—the next spot in the Volkov maneuver—had to be Dupont Circle, Four Acres Park. She'd run it by Winchester, and he'd agreed this could be it. He even joined in on the raid and was lurking out there too, somewhere in the shadows. But everyone had gotten into D.C. too early for the killer to have done anything, and so a stakeout it was.

But even Taylor was starting to feel antsy in her own skin. She spotted the other agents stationed across the park in their hiding positions—some behind trees, others behind monuments. Everyone was getting fidgety. They'd been here for hours, and each time they thought they saw someone—it became apparent very fast that it was just a person walking their dog, some teenagers out drinking late, or a person on a late-night run.

No one suspicious had turned up. Not yet.

But that didn't mean they wouldn't.

Maybe we spooked him, Taylor considered. The killer could have spotted an officer and backed off. But they were all carefully hidden, blending perfectly with the night itself; Taylor could only see them because she knew where to look. And chances were, this guy was doing all of his business at the least busy time of day—which would be between three and four a.m.

More minutes ticked on. Taylor checked her watch. 3:45 a.m.

Beside her, Calvin sighed in exasperation. "Sage," he whispered, "come on, how long are we gonna wait this out? I'm surprised Winchester hasn't already called it off…"

"Shh. Let's wait it out a bit longer." She stared into the dark, empty park, hoping for any movement. "He could still show up."

This was someone's *life* they were dealing with. And since the killer murdered the last victim on the scene, that meant he'd most likely do it again, so he'd be showing up with a live victim. A victim Taylor could save.

Her palms grew sweaty with anticipation as she stared and stared, willing the killer into existence. But there was only the stillness of night, the grass swaying in the gentle wind, a raccoon waddling through the park, the sound of crickets. All under the light of a half moon.

A murderer never showed. Not when it hit four a.m. Not fifteen after. In fact, no one entered the park at all.

A sudden voice appeared in Taylor's earpiece. It was Winchester.

"Okay, folks, it's negative. Let's call this off."

"What?" Taylor exclaimed. Around the park, the officers emerged from their hiding positions, stretching their limbs. Calvin did the same, yawning. But Taylor didn't have time to relax. Panic surged through her as she ran from the building across the street into the park as everyone merged together.

"No, go back, go back!" Taylor exclaimed. *Fuck!* If the killer didn't see them all before, he definitely would now. What was Winchester thinking?

The man himself appeared, looking exhausted with his hands on his hips. "Special Agent Sage," Winchester said, "this was a solid idea, don't get me wrong, but the guy's not coming. At least not tonight."

"We don't know that!" Taylor said, her voice trembling. She glanced around the empty park, looking beyond the perimeter to the streets surrounding. But not a single car passed. Not a soul was in sight.

Calvin appeared behind Taylor, and she looked to him to back her up—but he just shrugged, tired bags underneath his blue eyes, making his pale skin sallow. Taylor's heart sank. Once again, she felt like no one was on her side or trusting her gut instinct. Was this the betrayal Belasco had warned her about? It didn't feel big enough for the cards to pick up on, but it still hurt.

Winchester let out a long sigh. "Okay, Sage, here's the best I can offer. We'll leave two boys here to park and watch while the rest of us go home, or back to our damn hotels. Some of us have pretty long drives ahead of us. I'm with you on the theory, trust me, but we don't need a whole SWAT team here for it, okay?"

Taylor had already accepted that she was spending the night in D.C., and had rented a hotel in Dupont Circle. Calvin had done the same, at Taylor's request; she wanted him close by in case they made any big breaks in the case. She had hoped tonight would yield them bringing the killer in cuffed but, apparently, that wasn't going to happen.

"Well, I'll stay," Taylor said.

"No, Sage," Winchester said, "you need sleep. Both of you do. If anyone sees anything, we'll call you right away, got it?" Winchester's face hardened. "That's an order. I don't need my agents getting ill from overworking themselves. Go on, get out of here." He spun his finger around as he turned to walk away. "That goes for the rest of you too—let's head out."

Everyone departed from the park, leaving Taylor alone with Calvin. Defeat slammed on her shoulders. She couldn't accept that D4 wasn't right. She had been so sure of herself, and now she felt like a fool. Was it really all for nothing? She *still* couldn't even save one life?

A sudden light touch to her lower back pulled her from her trance. She glanced up at Calvin, who had a tired, but gentle smile on his face. "Sage, come on. We both need sleep, even if it's just a couple hours. Can't you rest even a little?"

Hugging herself, Taylor wanted to disappear. But she knew everyone was right. Her skin felt cold, and her eyelids were heavy and hurting. She probably needed sleep more than she even realized. Her mind could resist as much as she wanted, but her body was betraying her, and soon, she wouldn't be able to think as sharply either. And that wouldn't help her catch the killer.

"Okay," she resigned. "Let's go."

***

Taylor had tried to fall asleep—she really did. But thirty minutes later, she was still wide awake, staring at the stucco ceiling of her hotel room in Dupont Circle, unable to shake this case from her mind.

Maybe there could be a million other places in D.C. with the word "four" in them—but this one had seemed so perfect. So overly convenient. Maybe that was why it hadn't worked out. Things were never that easy for her: not in the last case, not in any of them before that either. Forget chess; it seemed like her whole life was a game of playing catch-up. Now, apparently, there was a serial killer trying to play a literal game with her—and she couldn't figure out his next damn move.

This was easily the most frustrating part of her job. The feeling of helplessness, uselessness, when she couldn't immediately solve something. Taylor knew she wasn't superhuman, but still, she held herself to a high standard. There were a few cases earlier in her career where she'd been able to track the killer a hell of a lot faster than she had with Jeremiah Swanson, and with this guy. Maybe she was being too hard on herself—but that was just her nature.

Then again, the obsession, she knew, was nothing but unhealthy.

She tossed and turned against the cold, stiff sheets of the hotel. Taylor never slept well away from her own bed, except at her parents' place, but that still felt like home. She shut her eyes again, images of the case flashing in her mind. She tried to will them down. Maybe even bury them beneath thoughts of Ben, if she had to. Her marriage was looking more and more doomed. Normally, Taylor tried not to think about it, but in this situation, the case was driving her madder than her unfortunate personal life.

But no matter how hard she tried, this time, it wasn't her husband who clawed to the forefront of her mind. It was that damn killer and whatever message he was trying to send.

Damn it, she cursed to herself. She couldn't stop thinking about it. Things earlier had felt so clean, like she'd been making true progress. The Volkov maneuver had to mean something. It was too deliberate. So either the killer was plotting his next move at a different D4 location, or there was something else Taylor was missing.

Anxious in her own skin, she snatched her phone off the nightstand and searched the Volkov maneuver again. She wanted to know the history of it. According to a Wikipedia page, it was coined by a man named Artemy Volkov, a chess grandmaster who had moved from Russia to America as a child. He was widely regarded as a young prodigy, a genius. There were a few pictures on his page; he was a frail man with buggy eyes and thinning hair, not much to look at.

Something about him seemed significant. Taylor kept scrolling, until she found a line that read:

Volkov now resides in Washington, D.C., where he continues his life as a grandmaster active in local tournaments.

Taylor's pulse jumped. She shot up in the bed. Not only was Volkov's literal signature on this string of murders—but he literally *lived* in D.C. How had she not seen this before? How did she not think to look?

She pushed that aside. Forget insecurity—this was a lead. She didn't think—she just dove out of her hotel room to Calvin's down the hall and knocked on the door, not caring if she was still in her pajamas, or if it was nearly five in the morning and the sun hadn't risen yet. This was huge. This guy, Artemy Volkov—he could literally *be* their killer. His prints were practically all over the case.

The hotel hallway was dark and quiet, and Taylor bounced on her feet as she waited for Calvin to answer. *Come on, Scott, where are you? Wake up!*

She knocked again. And again.

Until finally, a groggy voice from behind the door said, "Coming, coming…"

Calvin opened the door, rubbing his eye, and leaned against the doorframe. He was wearing a T-shirt and plaid pajamas. And while Taylor felt a zap of discomfort in seeing her partner in such an intimate way—and him seeing her—she didn't care. She burst into his dark room, despite his protests.

"Hey, Sage, what's going on?" he demanded.

Taylor flicked on the bedside lamp. Calvin sighed in exasperation, annoyance in his face as their eyes met. Taylor pulled out her phone and flashed Artemy Volkov's Wikipedia page at him.

"This guy, Volkov. He lives in D.C."

Calvin blinked, clearly still half-asleep. "Huh?"

"He *lives* here, Scott," Taylor said. "And his literal signature is on these crimes."

It seemed to clue in, and Calvin said, "Holy shit. You think he's our guy?"

"I think we have more than enough to get an emergency warrant on him, anyway," Taylor said.

She began to pace. Everything was falling into place. Talking to this Volkov *now* had to be their top priority; nothing else mattered.

"Okay," Calvin breathed out. "I'm with you. But it's five in the morning, Sage. It's gonna take a minute to get this all sorted out."

"We need to go now," Taylor said. "He could still have another victim."

Although Calvin had dark bags under his eyes, and his skin was paler than usual, he seemed to accept that he couldn't win this one.

Because he said, "I'll call and get that warrant. You figure out where he lives."

CHAPTER TWENTY ONE

When Taylor and Calvin pulled up outside of Artemy Volkov's house in Calvin's car, Taylor wasn't sure what would be more dangerous—the man himself, or the fact that she hadn't slept properly in days and her cognitive function was starting to show it.

She'd been okay earlier, her adrenaline high on the idea that Volkov was indeed their killer. But now that the sun was peeking over the roofs of the houses, Taylor's eyes were as heavy as mallets. And her mind was beginning to play tricks on her. With shaky limbs, Taylor got out of the passenger side of Calvin's car and nearly toppled over. Everything in her vision distorted for a moment.

Calvin hurried over to her. "Hey, you okay?"

Taylor straightened up as her head rush calmed. She didn't want Calvin to know how bad she was actually feeling; it would be weak, and it would only prove his point that she needed to rest rather than work on this case. But Taylor couldn't rest, not yet. Not until they caught him.

"I'm fine." She took a deep breath of cool morning air as she turned her gaze to Volkov's house. It was a bungalow with overgrown weeds on a lawn that looked like it hadn't seen a single shower all summer. Most of the windows were shielded by trees, and there was no car in the broken-up driveway.

The knot in Taylor's chest grew. Now wasn't the time to feel tired; there could be a killer in there. And her track record of confronting serial killers didn't exactly end in peaceful solutions. But unlike the last time, when she'd gone after Jeremiah Swanson, Calvin was with her. She wanted to take comfort in that, but every time she felt herself fully trusting him again, like she always had before, Belasco's warning slipped into her head. Before more paranoia could rack her brain, Taylor walked right up Volkov's driveway, Calvin close behind.

The front porch was shadowed, shielded by the tree that hid the front door, which had peeling brown paint. Taylor tried the doorbell. A slow ring ran through the inside of the house, but other than that, dead silence. So she knocked. No response.

"How long should we wait?" Calvin asked.

Taylor pounded on the door again, harder this time. Normally, she would give it a minute—maybe he was sleeping upstairs. But this was too pressing, and they already had the emergency warrant.

"Screw it," she said. "Let's go in."

She attempted to push the door open, but it was locked shut. Calvin took over, shoving his weight against the door and even trying to kick it, but it wouldn't budge.

"There's probably a glass door somewhere at the back," he said, huffing after he'd exerted himself. "Let's check it out."

They crept around the side of the house as the sun got higher in the sky, lighting up the disheveled backyard. It was even more overgrown and messy than the front yard. This place was creepy, Taylor thought as they made their way to the back, where a sliding glass door appeared to lead into the kitchen. Taylor peered through the glass—it was completely dark inside. No movement at all.

She looked at Calvin and nodded. He grabbed the handle of the door and lifted it up with all his weight, which successfully caused the door to be lifted from its locking mechanism. Calvin was able to slide the door open with ease, granting them access to the dark, quiet house.

Taylor's pulse increased as they entered. A strong smell—like soil and rotting food—made her stomach churn. And not only that, but as they stepped deeper into the kitchen, the light from the windows illuminated the piles of garbage that littered most of the floor. This guy's house made Joshua Smith's look clean. Artemy Volkov was clearly a hoarder.

"Hello, is anybody in here?" Calvin shouted out, hand on his gun. "This is the FBI. We have a warrant to search this property!"

His voice echoed through the house, but no one spoke back.

"He must not be here," Taylor said.

Calvin nodded. "Maybe not, but I'm gonna go clear the rooms to make sure. You stay here."

With that, Calvin disappeared into the house. Taylor remained in the kitchen, surrounded by garbage, before she snapped back to reality—she needed to look for clues.

Carefully stepping over the piles, she made her way out of the kitchen and into the living room. Bags of garbage piled up on the back wall, but this room had more floor space, and interestingly enough, the living room table was mostly cleared. The only thing that remained was a chess board next to a box.

Slowly, Taylor approached the box, and as she got closer, she made out the distinct shape of chess pieces thrown inside. With bated breath, she picked up one of them—a pawn—and smoothed her thumb along the surface, before she checked the bottom.

There was a distinct white V underneath the chess piece.

Everything stilled. Taylor had felt so sure Volkov was their guy.

But this actually proved it.

"Scott!" she shouted into the house. "Get down here!"

"Gimme a minute!" he called back.

Frantically, Taylor kept looking around for more clues in the mess of garbage. Paper after paper, useless junk thrown about.

And that was when she found it—a poster advertising a chess tournament this afternoon. It was in Richmond, Virginia, only two hours away.

Something moved behind her. Taylor jolted, startled, and turned to face the source of the sound—only to see Calvin entering the room, looking around in disgust.

"Man, this place needs a serious cleaning crew," he said. "But Volkov isn't here. No one is." When he saw the urgent look on Taylor's face, he immediately registered that she'd found something. "What is it, Sage?" he asked, stepping closer.

Taylor showed him the chess piece first. Calvin checked the bottom for the V and said, "Holy shit…"

"That's not all," Taylor said. She flashed him the poster. "I think I know where he'll be today."

***

"Sage, wake up."

Calvin's voice pulled Taylor from a dream. She opened her eyes to the windshield of his car, and her body felt stiff and sore from the position she'd been in. Confusion cluttered her mind as her consciousness returned; outside the car was a recreational building, and not only that, but it was clearly way later in the day, the sun much lower in the sky.

The car's clock read 2:56 p.m. The last thing Taylor remembered was that they had gotten on the road from Artemy Volkov's house at barely past six. How had she lost so much time?

"Scott, what's going on?" Taylor's skull pounded and her mouth was as dry as sand. A bottle of water appeared in her hand, and she glanced over at Calvin, who sat behind the wheel of the parked car. Taylor opened the cap and chugged some water back.

"You passed out the moment we started driving," Calvin said with a laugh.

"Christ, Scott, that was *hours* ago."

Taylor's mind raced. It was nearly five *fucking* p.m.—she had been out *all day.* An entire day of lost time. Hours and hours of work she could have done. She couldn't help it—her emotional side won, and frustration at her partner erupted.

"Why didn't you wake me up?" she asked him. "Scott, this is bad. Really bad. Why wouldn't you—"

"Taylor, relax."

It was rare he actually used her first name. Taylor scowled but kept quiet.

"You needed the rest," Calvin continued. "Hell, I slept for a bit too. But the most important thing is—we have eyes on Volkov." He nodded at the rec building across the parking lot from them. "He's in there. I just saw him go in myself."

"What happened?" Taylor was still frustrated that she hadn't been present.

"I reported everything we found," Calvin explained. "A crew is still over at Volkov's house, looking for more evidence and gathering DNA. But the chess pieces are a match, and Winchester is convinced this is our guy too. I made it clear to the boss that you and I are the ones going in to get him." Calvin's eyes softened, momentarily calming Taylor's nerves. "Sage, there was nothing you needed to be awake for—and I've never seen you that strung out. You needed sleep."

Taylor retreated into herself, feeling vulnerable and naked. It was true—she hadn't felt good at all, and admittedly now that she'd had some water, she felt much more clear-headed. Staying up until the crack of dawn and obsessing wasn't good for her. And even though she slept all day, thankfully, none of the fleeting dreams she could remember revolved around a nightmare.

I'm okay, she reminded herself.

And now it was time to finish her job. Well-rested and prepared. Sort of. She was still a bit disoriented, but this would have to do.

Getting out of the car, Taylor stretched her stiff limbs. It was warm outside, with a cool breeze in the late-summer air. Calvin got out and rounded the car with her. They stared ahead at the rec center, which had a stream of people piling into it.

Time to do this.

As Taylor and Calvin approached the rec center, Taylor considered their options for an approach. They already had more than enough to not only search the guy's property, but to arrest him too. She wasn't in the mood to beat around the bush, try to get him to talk—if anything, she was in more of a guns-blazing type of mood.

"Let's just arrest him," Taylor told Calvin as they neared the doors. "No need to play anymore games."

"I'm with you there," Calvin agreed.

They pulled their badges out and pushed past a hoard of people, into the rec center.

"Hey, excuse me!" an employee called after them, but Taylor just held up her badge, and the employee said nothing. The massive room was filled with tables and surrounding them were bleachers that were already almost full. Taylor had no idea chess brought out such a big crowd. Then again, Artemy Volkov was big enough in the community to have a Wikipedia page, so maybe they were really here to see him.

The entrance to the playing area was walled in by tables, where employees were admitting people who had tickets. Taylor and Calvin shoved their way to the front of the line, shouting, "FBI!"

Bystanders parted, gasping, as the two agents reached the entrance, badges still out. Taylor had sweat pooling at the base of her ponytail from the overwhelming heat of all these bodies packed together.

A young employee wearing a blue shirt with a chess piece on it wore a shocked expression as Taylor put her badge in her face. "Artemy Volkov. Is he here?"

"Uh, I—" the girl stammered. "He's playing, he's—"

"I need to speak to him now," Taylor said, looking over the top of the girl's head. She had seen pictures of Artemy not only on the internet, but hanging on the walls of his hoarder house, so she knew she was looking for a thin, sallow-faced man with a wisp of hair on his head.

Across table upon table, she zeroed in on him. Artemy Volkov, playing chess across from another person. Taylor pushed past the employee, into the playing area, with Calvin right behind her.

Artemy's eyes locked on them. For a moment, shock was written all over his face.

Then, he got up and ran.

Taylor barreled after him, her heart pounding. Artemy knocked over tables, sending chess pieces scattering as he made his escape.

Everyone was watching, startled and confused. A girl screamed as Artemy shoved her to the ground, but his thin body was betraying him—Taylor was drawing closer by the second.

Almost there. I've got you.

Volkov yelped as Taylor tackled him to the ground. He squirmed beneath her but lacked the strength to fight her off. In fact, pinning him felt more like holding down a scarecrow—the guy was remarkably thin and malnourished-looking, but that didn't mean he wasn't a killer. As she twisted his hands behind his back, she pulled her cuffs out.

"What is this?" he exclaimed, kicking, but Taylor had him pinned.

"Artemy Volkov," Taylor said, "you're coming with us."

She slapped the cuffs on his wrists.

CHAPTER TWENTY TWO

Taylor had seen the type of rage on Artemy Volkov's face before—he was like a rabid dog, shaking around in his chair as Taylor watched from outside of the interrogation room at Quantico. He reminded her of the many unhinged, weak men she'd arrested throughout her career. A small stature physically, likely compensated by a mental god complex. Volkov had been told he was a genius his whole life—surely, it had gone to his head.

Whether or not he was their killer was something she had yet to determine.

Calvin was just out getting the last bit of information from the techs on everything Volkov had done since he moved to America forty years ago. Taylor waited on him, even though she wanted nothing more than to storm in there and question Volkov herself.

Hugging herself, Taylor bit on her nail as she observed him, just as the door opened. She twirled around to see Calvin rushing in.

"Okay, so we don't have much, but what we do have is huge," he said. "Sage, Volkov *knew* victim two."

"What?" Taylor exclaimed. She hadn't seen that coming. Any doubts she had started to wash away. How could he both have the chess piece *and* have a connection to victim two without being the killer? "How?" she asked.

"Liam Stoll was a lawyer, right?" Calvin said. "Well, we found out that Volkov hired him a few years ago to help defend him in some defamation case. But Stoll lost, and Volkov blamed him."

"Shit," Taylor said. This was huge.

"Trust me, it doesn't end there," Calvin said. "A car matching his license plate was seen near Margot Withers's apartment in the days leading up to her murder. Not only that, but the team managed to access his internet history to find some truly disturbing—and illegal—stuff. This guy was doing some fucked-up shit."

Taylor wasn't surprised Volkov had guilt on him, but the amount they had found did shock her. Everything pointed to his guilt. If this was the case, and Volkov was the killer—that would make this one of the easiest arrests of her career. He'd barely put up a fight when she'd tackled him.

Calvin continued, "Volkov had used the dark web in an attempt to find someone to 'intimidate' one of his competitors into throwing a game of chess so Volkov could claim the prize himself. It never went anywhere, but still—the guy has a history of criminal behavior and a mountain of evidence against him." Calvin paused. "This is our guy."

Taylor couldn't deny the evidence. "Okay, let's get in there," she said. "I don't want to wait around anymore."

"Agreed," Calvin said.

With that, they both entered the interrogation room, where Volkov looked at them in disgust. "Can you people please fucking tell me what this is about?" he demanded.

Taylor and Calvin sat across from him casually.

"We'll get there," Calvin said.

With his face wrinkled, Volkov looked like a Shar Pei dog. Despite everything, Volkov was dressed fairly normally with a red plaid shirt and jeans—he reminded Taylor of an angry little man, but from the outside, no one would guess he was also a hoarder. And potentially a serial killer.

"Do you have any idea what you people have cost me?" Volkov ranted. "That tournament had a *five fucking thousand*-dollar prize. I needed that money, I—"

"If you sold some of the possessions in your home, you might have more to work with," Taylor muttered, not caring about being offensive or professional. Volkov was clearly a scumbag. There was so much dirt here that she didn't even know where to begin, and frustrated, she met his eyes.

"Okay, Artemy Volkov," she said, clasping her hands over the table. "We have a lot on you. So much it's making my head spin."

"A lot on me about *what?*" he demanded. Frustrated, he raked his thin fingers through his non-existent hair, then said: "Okay, if this is about that Farris guy—look, I just wanted someone to scare him, all right? Nothing more, nothing less, now can you let me out of these things?"

Taylor lifted a brow. Wait, he was confessing to the dark web thing without being prompted? Farris was presumably the name of the guy Volkov was attempting to intimidate.

Exchanging a perplexed look with Calvin, Taylor said, "We know about Farris, yes. We know about your interest in illegal services via the dark web." Her eyes hardened on him. "We also know about Margot Withers, Liam Stoll, and Michael West."

"Who?" Volkov scowled at her like she was an idiot. "Stoll? For fuck's sake—what's he got to do with this? And I don't know any Margret or Michaels."

"Margot," Taylor corrected, irritated. He killed her and he wouldn't even say her name right? The disrespect caused a pool of anger to boil in her.

But it also planted a seed of doubt. Taylor looked hard into Volkov's eyes. She saw a pathetic and small man. Someone who'd cheat to win, just like George Fields. But were these the eyes of a deadly murderer? Taylor couldn't tell.

Taylor decided to dial it back. He was admitting to the Liam Stoll connection, so she asked, "But you know Liam Stoll."

Volkov rolled his eyes. "That guy is a hack."

"What makes you say that?" Taylor asked.

"I hired him to help defend me in a defamation lawsuit and we lost." Bitterness rolled off Volkov's tongue. "And he wasn't cheap, either."

"But you do know Liam Stoll was murdered," Taylor said. It was not a question.

Confusion cluttered Volkov's wrinkled face. "What?"

"He was murdered," Taylor repeated. "You knew that."

"No, I did not *know that,*" Volkov spat back. "Who nailed him? Another dissatisfied customer?"

Taylor and Calvin both stared at Volkov, waiting for it to register.

And when it did, all the color drained from his face.

"Wait—you think *I* did it? I haven't even seen that guy in over a year—why the hell would I get him now? And if I was going to, don't you think I would've tried the dark web again? Because I would have. If you think I'd risk going to prison over that hack, you're dead wrong."

Taylor observed him. It was probably one of the calmer, more rational reactions to an accusation she'd ever seen. And in all honesty, it sort of made sense—Volkov did have a clear history of using the dark web. But this wasn't just one murder or an act of revenge—it was a game he was playing, and maybe he wanted to dirty his own hands. Maybe he wouldn't trust someone else to do his moves for him.

But despite everything—all of the evidence—Taylor had one of those gut feelings again. With everything pointing to Volkov, why didn't Taylor believe he was actually the killer?

Beside her, Calvin cleared his throat. "Okay, let's just cut the shit, Volkov. We know you killed Liam Stoll. Margot Withers and Michael West too. You were near Margot's apartment days before she died, and we found chess pieces in your home that are an exact match to the ones we found at the crime scenes."

"What?" Volkov retorted. "My chess pieces? Do they have a V on them? Because I'm missing those, and—"

"You know there's a V on them because you put them there," Calvin snapped. He was showing uncharacteristic irritation—being aggressive with Volkov hadn't been part of their game plan, but she didn't object. Whatever got the guy to confess. If he did confess, maybe then Taylor could get rid of the suspicion that they were wrong about the killer yet again.

"I didn't!" Volkov shouted. Now, he was starting to sweat, his eyes nervously darting around. "I didn't, someone stole the pieces from me! They've been missing for weeks! I've never killed anyone!"

"You did," Calvin said. "A3. B4. C2. That's your move, isn't it?"

Volkov scrambled to reply, but Calvin wasn't done. He stood up, pressed his palms flat on the table, and leaned over Volkov, who stared up at him, bug-eyed.

"You murdered those people as part of a sick, twisted game that you wanted us to play, but we're cutting you off, Volkov. You're gonna rot in a cell for what you did."

Calvin's sudden behavioral shift made Taylor's head spin. She looked up at him, partially in awe of his vigor, but also slightly irritated—she had wanted to speak to him calmly first, but now the tension in the room was like a rubber band about to snap.

"We're done here," Calvin said.

Standing up, he briskly approached the door, and Taylor shot one more look at a flabbergasted Volkov before she followed after. As much as she wanted to interrogate Volkov, she also wanted to know what Calvin's outburst was all about.

Once outside of the interrogation room, Calvin's face was still red, and Taylor scowled at him.

"Scott, what the hell was that? Why are you so angry?"

"I'm just sick of it," he said, pacing. "I'm sick of twisted fucks like him lying and wasting our time. We know he did it. He has no alibi for any of the murders and we've got so much evidence a child could solve this case. So why even bother entertaining him and questioning him? Let's just throw him in a cell for the rest of his life and call it a day."

Taylor could understand that. And the more Calvin spoke, the surer Taylor was that she couldn't vocalize her own doubts about Volkov's guilt. She knew it was questionable, and she couldn't quite explain it herself. It was one of those gut feelings that there was more to this case than met the eye. But the last time Taylor had expressed such doubts—even though she was right in the end—no one believed in her. She didn't want to experience that rejection again.

Belasco's warning swam through her mind. The betrayal. Maybe this would be it. Maybe this time, Taylor needed to get some evidence before she came out with a new theory. If she could prove that she wasn't crazy first—to herself, as well—then she hoped Calvin would back her up without resistance.

Just then, a jovial Winchester entered the room. "Here's my finest agents! You two did it again, didn't you?" He slapped them each on the shoulder once.

Calvin laughed, trying to calm down. "Yes, sir. We got him."

"And in record time too." Winchester's eyes fell on Taylor. "Sage, I knew getting you in here was gonna be worth it, but you continue to exceed my expectations. You and Agent Scott make a fine team."

Taylor nodded obediently, hoping her face didn't give her true thoughts away. "Thank you, sir."

"We have more than enough to book this guy," Winchester went on. "He's a real creepy fellow too. Just the pictures of that house of his made me wanna throw up my lunch."

"You should have smelled it, sir," Calvin joked.

"I'll pass on that one, Scott." Grabbing both of their shoulders, Winchester smiled. "You two have earned yourselves a night off. Go on and relax, will ya? We'll take over from here."

"Thank you, sir," both Taylor and Calvin said as Winchester left the room.

Taylor gazed back into the glass leading to the interrogation room, where Volkov had gone limp around his chair, like he'd accepted his defeat.

"You heard the boss, Sage," Calvin said, breaking Taylor's reverie. She met his eyes. "You should go home and celebrate with your husband. I'll do the same. With my cat."

Taylor forced a smile and nodded. But of course, Taylor wouldn't be able to relax after a day like this; not a chance. She would go home, yes, but it sure as hell wouldn't be to celebrate.

The work wasn't over yet. Not for her.

Maybe it never would be.

CHAPTER TWENTY THREE

She was everything he'd ever wanted and more. The perfect addition to his set—the perfect queen to rule his game.

Sitting in his car, the grandmaster admired the poster of her spread on his lap as he was parked on a dark, quiet street. THE QUEEN OF U-STREET was plastered in a bold font across the top with a picture of his queen, red-lipped and stunning, smiling at the camera as she wore a chef's hat. He lifted his head to peer outside of the window, where at the restaurant across the street, he saw her: his queen, looking just as radiant as in the photo.

Inside the restaurant, he could see her furiously working in the kitchen, her brows pinched. He imagined sweat was pooled beneath that hat. She'd look much better in a crown, but this worked too. It was just such a shame he would have to sacrifice her. In the past couple of days that he'd been watching her, he had to admit, he'd grown strangely fond of the way she ruled over that kitchen like a true monarch.

But dinner service would be done soon, and tonight was the night. She would be put toward another cause, a more worthy cause. The kitchen would find another ruler, but she—she was his. He deserved her more than they did.

Minutes ticked on as the grandmaster watched the kitchen close, and his queen began her nightly closing ritual. Putting away the prep. Wiping down the stations. She was the type of girl to get her hands dirty along with her subjects instead of letting them do all the work. He admired that about her. He hoped she was enjoying her last night.

Soon, the restaurant lights went dim. She would be leaving out the back door in about fifteen minutes to her car in the parking lot. Turning on his vehicle, he pulled out of his parking spot on the street and geared around to the back of the building, where some of her subjects were getting into their cars and leaving. She was always the last to go.

He waited until the last car was gone before he pulled into the parking lot and hid behind a dumpster. He turned off his car and got out, into the cool night, and breathed in deep. It smelled so clean at this end of town. So much different from his. Even when he was right behind the barrels of trash her restaurant had thrown out during the evening, it was still better than the life he'd been given. A touch of jealousy and anger flared up in him; why did other people, stupider people, less deserving people, end up with more money than him? The lavish cars, the big houses—they didn't deserve them. He did.

But he stifled those thoughts down as best as he could. Tonight wasn't about negative emotions—it was about winning.

And win, he would.

Peeking around the corner of the dumpster, he saw her car was still there. He hid from sight again and waited for the sound. His heart thrummed slowly in his chest, the anticipation building.

This will get their attention. Those foolish police officers. They knew nothing about the game; he'd made three moves now, and not one person had caught on or responded. What was he, invisible? Why couldn't they see him?

All it meant was that he needed to be bolder. Stronger. Show them what he was truly made of. Tonight, he would do things differently. He would do something they couldn't ignore.

He would move his queen.

At long last, the sound he was hoping for struck like a heavenly chord in his ear: the back door of the restaurant opening. Her keys jingled as she closed up. Then, the soft sound of her feet scuffled against the concrete as she moved across the parking lot to her car.

He peeked around the dumpster. Like all the other times, she had her eyes glued to her cellphone, catching up on notifications as she idly walked to her vehicle. Perfect. She wouldn't even notice him coming.

But he had to act fast. Sucking in a breath, he crept out from behind the dumpster and descended upon his queen. She was still looking at her phone as he drew closer, and closer, and closer—

He grabbed her and knocked her on the back of the head. Instantly, she fell from grace like a sack of potatoes. He smirked. He was getting too good at this.

Feeling satisfied, accomplished, he dragged her back to his car, letting her cell phone stay in the parking lot. Where they were going, she wouldn't need it.

Once at his car, he opened up the passenger door to introduce her to her new throne. Her final thrown. To treat her with the dignity she deserved, he delicately positioned her in the car and put on her seatbelt.

Now, the game could continue.

CHAPTER TWENTY FOUR

Taylor finally walked through the front door of her house, feeling like she hadn't been home in eons. It was true, she'd spent the last two nights away, and she wouldn't have minded a third. But she needed to be home to work in her own space, and she wasn't about to let the tension with Ben impede her ability to crack this case. If there was anything left to crack at all.

Still, Taylor had called Ben ahead to let him know she'd be home tonight so he could mentally prepare, or even leave, if he wanted to. Taylor expected the latter, to be honest. Which was why it surprised her that as she was kicking off her shoes, a smell wafted to her nose. Garlic butter and squash.

Sounds—like pans simmering and plates being moved—came from the kitchen, as well. Taylor needed to get downstairs to her office, but her curiosity won, and she peered into the dining room just in time to see Ben spooning out servings of mashed squash next to juicy-looking steaks. There were two plates out.

He'd cooked for her.

Stunned, Taylor stood like a deer caught in the headlights until Ben glanced up at her. It wasn't exactly joy that filled his stare, but at the very least, he smiled. She smiled back.

"Hey, you're here," he said.

"As promised," Taylor muttered. She glanced at the door leading to the basement. The urge to get down there was strong. But how could she now? Maybe if she wanted to completely destroy her marriage, she could reject Ben's meal, but she didn't have the heart. He was trying to make amends—what else could Taylor ask for? If she wanted to fix things, she had to put in at least some effort.

Even when a killer might still be out there? her conscience said, but Taylor pushed it aside.

"Come on, sit," Ben said. "Everything's ready. You're right on time."

"Ah, okay." Awkwardly, Taylor took her usual spot on the left side of the table while Ben took the right. The plate looked delicious—Ben had always been a fantastic and creative cook. The steak complemented the garlicy squash, and Taylor's mouth watered. It had been a bit since she'd had a proper meal.

"I hope you like it," Ben said. The niceness felt forced, but Taylor nodded, taking a tiny bite of her squash.

"It's delicious," she said honestly.

Ben began slicing his steak, which broke apart like butter. "So, how's your case going?"

Taylor hesitated. Ben knew she hated talking about work at the dinner table. But she also knew that Ben hated being so shut out of her life.

"Well, we arrested someone today," Taylor said, taking a small bite of steak, thinking back to the interrogation of Volkov. Something just didn't sit right with it. Why admit to one crime, but not the others? Based on the trail the killer had left so far, Taylor sensed he was a cryptic, calculating type—someone with a god complex, who thought people were just chess pieces there for *his* game, for *his* amusement, for *his* ends.

Volkov was potentially calculating, but he seemed too flabbergasted by the accusations. He lacked the delusional arrogance Taylor would expect from someone like this. Taylor felt certain that whoever the killer was wanted attention more than anything; he wanted a game. Maybe, in a sick and twisted way, he even wanted to get caught.

"Let me guess," Ben cut in when Taylor didn't finish. "You don't think he's your guy?"

Taylor nodded. Maybe it would help to tell someone. Even if it was just Ben. "It just doesn't feel right."

"Well, aren't you normally right on these things?" Ben suggested. "You were right last time."

"Yes, but… it's complicated."

"How so?"

Taylor felt uncomfortable under the weight of the question. She took a sip of white wine to calm her nerves. She'd let Ben in a little—wasn't that enough? "Maybe we can skip the work talk on my end," she said with a laugh. "How's the hotel coming along?"

Ben gave her a tight-lipped smile. "Good. Construction is ready to be underway. We're hoping to have everything finished by November, at the latest, which is ambitious for such a large-scale project, but it's gonna work out."

"That's great, honey."

Silence. More awkwardness filled the air. Taylor hadn't thought twice about calling Ben "honey"—it was instinct. But as soon as the word left her mouth, she regretted it. It didn't feel right, and judging by the look on Ben's face, he didn't like it either.

As they sat together, quietly finishing their meals, they didn't feel like husband and wife at all. And as much as it hurt Taylor's heart, she couldn't shake the feeling that things really were different between them. Maybe they always would be.

She poked at her food, and memories of their first date together surfaced in her mind.

After convincing her to give him her number at that work party at the bar, Ben had called Taylor and arranged for them to go on a date at an incredibly ritzy steakhouse. He didn't seem rich by any means, and Taylor remembered thinking that she would offer to at least pay half, as the place was far from cheap—some of the meals were forty dollars a pop.

But it was delicious, too, and they'd had a great time. She could barely remember the topics of their conversation, just that he'd talked her ear off, and she'd been thoroughly amused by his banter and humor. It felt like it'd been so long since he'd cracked a joke with her like that.

The night had ended beautifully too. As he'd walked her back to her car, they'd shared short, but sweet and simple kiss under the stars. Taylor remembered thinking, in that very moment, that nothing had ever felt so right for her.

Ben Chambers was her future. Maybe she didn't realize it quite like that at the time, but her heart seemed to know that one day they'd get married.

And of course, they did. And things were happy… until recently. Taylor was still waiting for Ben to ask her how *she* was feeling about her infertility through all of this. But she was starting to think that would never happen.

Absentmindedly, Taylor finished her food. The moment her plate was cleared, Ben picked it up and took it to the kitchen, rinsing it off and leaving it in the sink. Taylor waited at the dining table—they still had wine left, and maybe he wanted to finish it with her. Maybe they could address this giant elephant in the room like two rational adults. But he picked up his glass and pivoted toward the living room, where he could cross to reach the stairs.

"Where are you going?" Taylor asked.

"I'm gonna finish this up and read before bed," he said. "I can tell you still have work to do. Good luck, okay?"

"Wait," she said.

Ben faced her.

Nerves rose in her, but she just came out with it: "Ben, maybe we should talk about, you know…"

He averted his eyes. A heavy pause hung in the air before he finally replied. "That's okay. Another night. You're busy, and I'd like to finish this book."

Taylor just nodded, even though annoyance flushed through her. She understood Ben hadn't consented to a childless marriage, but Taylor hadn't consented to a marriage that lacked all communication. Yes, she'd messed up by not telling him the truth. She'd owned that. But now that it was on the table, was it so crazy for her to think she and her husband could talk about it?

She decided it wasn't worth her time right now to go after him, to be angry with him. She did have more work to do, and this had been enough of a distraction.

Once Ben was gone, Taylor shot back the rest of her wine before she went into her office downstairs, comforted by the silence, the only sound a calm white noise from their air conditioner grumbling. She sat down at her desk and set up her laptop.

First thing's first: she reviewed all the case files. Every image, every piece of evidence, every photo taken of the bodies. Then, she considered everything she knew so far about potential next moves—the Volkov maneuver had seemed so promising, but even now, no body had dropped in a D4 location. They still could, but ideally, Taylor could get ahead of this before that had to happen.

Still, the Volkov maneuver being used had to be significant. But if the killer really was Volkov, why would he put his own signature on it? It was too easy. Too obvious. Then again, there was also the issue of the matching chess pieces. Taylor couldn't deny that evidence was enough to put Volkov behind bars.

I have to be missing something, she thought. And sitting here in her basement, staring at her computer, wasn't giving her any bright ideas. She checked the time.

The chess tournament was nearing its end. But it wasn't over yet.

The idea struck Taylor quickly, and she abruptly stood up to gather her things.

Richmond was a hell of a lot closer than D.C. So if Taylor got on the road now, she might make it there before the rec center shut down.

Maybe it was a shot in the dark, but someone there could still know something.

***

Taylor barely arrived on time. Bursting through the doors of the rec center, she saw the bewildered faces of the employees who'd witnessed her arrest of Artemy Volkov earlier that day. They all look slightly scared, as if she were back for more blood, and any of them could be her next victim.

But Taylor was only interested in one person—the killer. He was the only one who needed to worry.

Some employees were clearing away the tables from the main area when Taylor approached with her badge out, despite most people seeming to recognize her. Two teenagers—a boy and a girl—were carrying away a table, and they gawked at Taylor, so she chose them first.

"Hi there," Taylor said.

The two muttered, "Hi," back as they slowly dropped the table.

"Do you mind if I ask you a few questions?" Taylor asked, hands on her hips as she caught her breath. She'd was still reeling from dashing across the parking lot to make it in here in time.

"Is it about Volkov?" the boy blurted. "'Cause we saw him get arrested earlier and it was totally crazy."

"Crazy," the girl echoed with an eager nod.

That was one way to put it. Volkov's arrest had been very public, so it didn't surprise her they'd still be curious about it.

"Right," Taylor said. "Artemy Volkov is currently still in custody."

"What'd he do?" the boy asked.

Of course, Taylor couldn't share details of the case with them. But she was interested in what they might have to say. "What do you think?" she asked, genuinely curious.

The two teenagers looked at each other, before the girl said, "He probably tried to scare someone again."

"Again?" Taylor asked. "Does Volkov have a history of violence here?"

"Not violence," the guy said. "He just likes to blabber on a lot, you know, ranting. He's pretty old, so..."

Taylor nodded. It seemed anything they had to say about Volkov wouldn't be helpful, but also, Volkov wasn't the one Taylor wanted—they already had him. What she really wanted to know was if there was anyone else in the chess scene who had a reputation.

She asked, "Has there been anyone else around this tournament at all, anyone who might strike you as strange?"

"I dunno." The teenage boy shrugged.

"We're just the cleanup crew," the girl said. "We don't like, play chess."

Of course, Taylor thought bitterly. "Can you point me to someone who knows everyone around here?"

They pointed toward a group of people, all wearing the same T-shirt as the teenagers, only theirs were different colors. They glanced at Taylor as she noticed them, and when they saw her eyes on them, they looked away. She approached as they awkwardly shifted around on their heels, as though waiting for her. Taylor recognized one of them as the employee she'd brushed past right before Volkov's arrest.

"Hey, everyone," Taylor said. "You mind if I ask a few questions?"

They all nodded, muttering awkwardly.

Taylor said, "Earlier today, the FBI obtained an arrest warrant for one of the competitors here, Artemy Volkov. Some of you may have witnessed that."

They all nodded, exchanging fearful looks.

Taylor wasn't sure how much of the case she should divulge. But what she did want is for them to know how serious this was. She was getting desperate, and the reason for Volkov's arrest would be made public soon anyway—especially if the FBI planned to pin him as the killer.

"Volkov has been arrested under suspicion of murder," Taylor said.

Now, everyone's demeanor changed from uncomfortable to shocked as they all exchanged words, like, "What?" and "Seriously?"

"Murder?" one girl asked. "There's no way… really?"

"You don't think he's capable of that?" Taylor asked.

Half of them shrugged. Half said nothing.

In order to dig up more, Taylor needed to give a bit more. They couldn't help her based off nothing. But she had a strong gut feeling something here could lead her down the right path. With all these "gut feelings," Taylor bitterly thought she was starting to sound like Belasco, which was ridiculous. Yet still, if she didn't see his one through, and another body did drop… she'd never forgive herself.

Her father had always taught her to trust her intuition. More often than not, Taylor had been right. She had to persevere.

So she said, "The case we're working on has links to the world of chess. That's why we're here."

One employee, a man in a red T-shirt with a chess piece on it, stammered, "But didn't you already arrest Volkov?"

"We did. But only under suspicion."

"So maybe he didn't do it," one girl said. It was the same one Taylor had encountered earlier that day—a short young woman with brown hair, tied back in a messy ponytail.

Taylor thought carefully on her response. "We're open to exploring alternative options. If you can think of anyone else around the tournament who has maybe struck you as odd, out of place, or potentially violent, please let me know."

The group looked around at each other, clueless, then each muttered, "Sorry."

They didn't know anything.

Taylor sighed. Another dead end.

"Okay," she said. "Thank you for your time, anyway." She handed them each a card. "If you think of anything, please let me know. I'm Special Agent Taylor Sage, and I can be reached twenty-four-seven."

As Taylor walked away, the group dispersed as well, splitting up to go get ready to leave. But Taylor glanced over her shoulder to see that the girl with the ponytail was still standing there, looking at Taylor's card. Almost like she had something more to say.

They locked eyes. Taylor turned toward her, just as the girl seemed to make up her mind and came jogging over.

"Um, actually," she began, "there is someone."

Taylor's ears perked. This could be something. "Oh?"

"There was this guy—he was a chess prodigy named Gabe French. He was one of the best, even though he was pretty young. Only eighteen when he was around. Maybe he's nineteen now."

A bit younger than what Taylor would expect. But it wasn't impossible.

"A lot of people seem to have totally forgotten about this," the girl said, "but about a year ago, at our last major tournament, he lost to the Volkov maneuver, to Volkov himself."

Taylor's heart raced. This was going somewhere. She thought of the matching chess pieces, one of the biggest pieces of evidence the

FBI had. If the real killer knew Volkov, he could have stolen the pieces from him.

And if he knew Volkov's maneuver, he could have used it to lay out the victims intentionally.

It's a frame job. All the pieces were clicking into place. But the employee had more to say.

"It was during finals," the girl continued, "and they were the last two competitors playing for the grand prize. When Gabe lost, he screamed in rage and flipped a table. He told Volkov he'd make him pay. But that was the last time any of us saw him. He completely disappeared."

"And you heard nothing else about him?" Taylor asked.

"Never," she said. "I heard he got suspended, but it was only for a few months, so when he didn't come back, it was really weird. He was always an angry kid. Really moody. But chess was his life. I assumed he went to play somewhere else."

Everything fell into place around Taylor. If her gut feeling told her before that Volkov wasn't their guy—it was now telling her that Gabe French had to be him. He had to be.

"Thank you," she said to the girl, pivoting toward the exit. No matter how she felt, she knew it wasn't enough to convince Winchester to get a warrant. Let alone an emergency warrant. "Gut feelings" didn't hold up in court, and Taylor would have to gather some proof first.

She ran as fast as she could back to her car. *Time to hunt this Gabe French guy down.*

CHAPTER TWENTY FIVE

Taylor's headlights sliced through the darkness of the street, illuminating a garbage can at the side of the house Gabe French lived in. According to the database, he rented a basement apartment at this very location on the outskirts of D.C. The deeper Taylor had descended into this neighborhood, the more uneasy she had felt—it was far from nice, and his house resembled more of a dilapidated shack than a warm home. The window of the upper level was broken in and shielded off by a garbage bag that fluttered in the nighttime wind.

In her quick research, Taylor had learned that the upstairs apartment had been occupied by heroin addicts who had overdosed and died on the premises little more than two months ago. The landlords hadn't filled the apartment yet, and judging by the damage, it didn't look like they were about to.

The basement apartment, though, had not been condemned, and Gabe French reportedly still rented it. Taylor parked her car at the side of the road, taking a deeper look at the house. No car in the driveway. If Gabe was indeed their killer, then chances are, he had a vehicle to move those bodies around in. So maybe he wasn't home.

That wasn't necessarily a good thing. For one, it meant he could be out there, hunting a victim right now—or worse. But if he wasn't there, then Taylor did have the advantage of raiding his house without him there to put up a fight.

Only one way to find out. With her heart pounding, Taylor exited the safety of her car and landed on the quiet street. She tried to be silent, but even the click of her door shutting behind her stirred something at the house across the street. Taylor startled at a rustling sound and spun around. A skunk waddled out from a bush, sniffing the grass. She let out a breath.

Clearly, she was too jumpy to be doing her job at full capacity, but that wasn't about to stop her. *Show time, Sage. Let's keep it together.*

Ducked down low, Taylor crept up to the house and moved along the side. A small, rectangular window was built into the foundation of the house near the back, and Taylor knelt down so she could peek inside, where it was too dark to make out anything concrete. She checked over her shoulder—no one was there, so Taylor carefully lowered to the ground so she could get a closer look through the window.

With her nose practically pressed to the glass, Taylor squinted to see. She made out the form of a messy kitchen, and across the chaos, a small, square-shaped table with a single chair.

And on the table, Taylor swore she saw chess pieces. She squinted to see clearer.

It was actually a full board, and only one side of the map had moved—the black side. Even though white always went first, Gabe had chosen black. Maybe he felt it better represented him than white—more like darkness.

As she took a closer look at the board, she noted the way the pieces on his half had moved—and they lined up exactly in the way the Volkov maneuver dictated.

A queen had shifted into D4 too.

Taylor began trembling again, her mind running a mile a minute. If he had made his D4 move—did that mean he had his victim?

Had he already killed them?

Her pulse jumped as she stood up and pressed her back to the brick wall. It seemed like nobody was home, but she needed to get in there.

Taylor paused for a moment to consider her options. So, she was here—but she was also alone, about to enter the den of a potentially dangerous serial killer. She might now have enough to convince Calvin something was at play here—but then again, as far as she knew, Belasco's prediction had still not come to fruition. Which meant it still could.

Could this be the moment he betrays me?

Taylor couldn't answer that. Maybe Belasco couldn't, either. But at the very least, she needed his backup. After what happened last time with Jeremiah Swanson, Taylor needed someone to know where she was; it was too dangerous otherwise, and she was done recklessly risking her life. Well, to a degree, anyway.

She called his cellphone, eyes flicking around the trees that fenced in the back of the house. The backyard was just as disheveled as the front, with patches of dead grass littered everywhere and weeds overgrown. The phone rang and rang. Calvin didn't answer, but it went to voicemail. Better than nothing.

"Scott," Taylor whispered into the phone, "I've made a major breakthrough in the case. Artemy Volkov isn't the killer. I'm at someone's house—Gabe French, an old rival of Volkov's with a violent history, who I'm certain is trying to frame him for the murders, or at least send Volkov a message. He could still kill again." She stopped, took a breath. "I'm entering his apartment, Scott. I'll text you the address. Just—get here. Please."

With that, Taylor hung up, texted Calvin the address, then faced the stairs that led down to the door of Gabe's basement apartment. Taylor's hands were shaking, and when she caught herself, she closed her eyes and took a moment. *One. Two. Three.*

You can do this.

When she opened her eyes again, her brave face was on. Taylor went to the stairs and descended. Cigarette butts were littered everywhere, making the drain at the bottom of the concrete stairwell blackened. The door to the apartment was peeling, and through the window, it was pitch black. Taylor knocked anyway.

And again.

But no one answered.

She didn't have time to get a warrant. And she didn't know if Calvin would ever call back—by then, Gabe could be home, and it could be over. Now was her only chance.

Taylor pulled two bobby pins out from her hair and straightened them. Although this door didn't look like it would need much convincing to open, Taylor didn't feel like barreling in the way Calvin would have. After some finagling, she was able to pop open the lock, and the door creaked open, revealing the empty house.

A stale smell reached Taylor's nose. As she stepped inside, more dust assaulted her nostrils—she had to cover her face to avoid coughing. But she was in. And she was alone. But she had to move quickly, before he got back.

Using the flashlight on her phone, Taylor began navigating Gabe's apartment. And what she found was nothing short of tragic. There was a dust-coated display case filled with picture frames, all of Gabe throughout the years—him with a huge smile, crowned the winner of a tournament when he was only eight years old. Pictures of him as he grew older, still a chess champion, well on his way to greatness. Eventually, Gabe grew into an awkward teenager, and the photos started showing a smug, more arrogant vision of him. He no longer looked proud and accomplished to win—he looked like he felt he deserved it. Like it was owed to him.

Where were his parents in all of this? Taylor hadn't had much time to do recon on his life when she was digging up his address, but she did read that he was an orphan. Grew up in the system. In and out of foster care, but a chess prodigy who was taken under the wing of his teachers. Things went downhill after high school, but he got his own place. It was cheap, but as Taylor could see for herself, dingy, unclean, and frankly, unhealthy. This was no place for an adolescent to live.

The pictures eventually stopped. It seemed he hadn't added one in quite a while. Maybe getting suspended from the tournament after losing to Volkov was his fall from grace, and he'd been on this downward spiral ever since.

Taylor could tell based on the state of his life. The kitchen sink was piling with dishes. There was random clutter everywhere. Even if Gabe hated Volkov—they had more in common than he probably realized. Creeping through the house, Taylor noticed the cobwebs collecting in the corners, and that the smell of rot and garbage seemed to follow her no matter what.

In the kitchen, she found the table with the chess pieces on it. She took a picture of the board. Then, panicking, she looked around for anything that might signal where he could be now—a poster, a flier, anything at all. But she found useless clutter, random papers and reports of unpaid bills, envelops that were never opened. Scrambling, she ran into the next room, and that was where she saw it: a dual monitor computer, set up right beside a smelly, unmade bed.

In the darkness of the house, the computer tower's light slowly blinked, causing the room to flash red as she made her way toward it. With bated breath, she sat down at the rickety office chair and tapped the keyboard to open the computer. It loaded a password-protected screen. Taylor typed in something random—Volkov—but it didn't work. The screen offered a hint, and Taylor clicked it:

V3.

Taylor typed 'Volkovmaneuver' next, but no dice. She tried again with different capitalization, but nothing worked.

A message popped up: ONE MORE ATTEMPT LEFT UNTIL LOCKDOWN.

Fuck. She had to think carefully. V had to be Volkov…

Could the '3' signify something? An idea popped into her head. Readying her fingers over the keyboard, she licked her lips and tried again:

A3B4C2.

The first three moves of the Volkov maneuver.

The screen opened. Taylor's heart jumped.

She was in.

A blank desktop was spread before her. Taylor didn't know where to start. She checked over her shoulder, into the empty house, feeling like someone could pop out at any minute. But she was still alone. And she had her gun—she needed to focus.

The best place to start had to be the internet. His search history could tell her everything. Taylor opened the browser and checked it. His last searches revolved around one person: Harriet Fleming. One of the last articles he'd read was called THE QUEEN OF U-STREET. Harriet was head chef at a restaurant called Arpeggio. For her young age, it seemed she had an impressive track record. A pretty, white-toothed woman smiled at Taylor through the screen as she scrolled the page.

This was it. His next victim. His "Queen."

Taylor shuddered. Okay, so she had his potential next victim. But where was he taking her? She needed to streamline this process—she didn't have all night to weed through his entire history. If she could narrow down the subject to searched locations, maybe she could get a clue. So she opened Google Maps and typed into the search bar. Taylor scanned the last. He had looked up the location of Arpeggio's, which was downtown D.C.

And four other locations stood out, starting from the bottom.

The US Capitol parking lot.

The Before You Go travel agency.

C-2-IT staffing agency.

And lastly: Dupont Circle, Four Acres Park.

Taylor's eyes widened. She couldn't believe what she was seeing. She had been right about the location—just not the *time.* And after Volkov's arrest, the patrol car at Four Acres had been released. Which meant no one was guarding it, and Gabe French was free to kill his victim there.

She ripped herself out of the computer chair; whatever else Gabe had on here, the police would raid later. Right now, she had to save a life. There was still time.

There had to be.

CHAPTER TWENTY SIX

As Taylor's car whipped away from Gabe French's house—destination: Dupont Circle—she hastily dialed Calvin again, popping her phone on speaker as she drove. Biting her lip, she waited for the ring, praying she'd get through to him.

This time, Calvin picked up on the second ring.

"Sage, I was just—"

"Scott, where are you?" She didn't have time to waste. But it was good to hear his voice.

"I'm just arriving in D.C.," he said. "I'm on my way to the address you sent me."

"Change of plans," Taylor said. "He's taking a victim to Four Acres Park. I saw it on his computer."

"Okay, I'm only five minutes away."

Taylor checked the name of the intersection she pulled up to. "I can make it in ten."

"No problem. I'll wait for you."

"Got it. The parking lot across from Four Acres." She paused. "But keep an eye out, okay?"

"Understood," Calvin said. "See you soon."

With that, they hung up, and Taylor gripped the steering wheel until her knuckles turned white. It was nearly midnight—still early enough for people to be about, so it was unlikely Gabe would kill his victim yet. But surely, he was plotting it. Maybe lurking near the location, considering he wasn't home. Taylor trusted Calvin to get there and keep an eye out before he could make a move.

Gabe could be anywhere. And now that Taylor knew, one hundred percent, that he was the killer, she wanted nothing more than to teleport right there before it was too late. Maybe it already was too late—but either way, she needed to act fast.

She pressed her foot on the gas pedal and began ducking and weaving through traffic. Federal agent or not, she couldn't afford to get pulled over, so she had to stay tame. But that left her with about eight minutes ahead of her to do nothing but ruminate.

As she got stuck behind a red light, frustration burned into her. And now that she was alone with her thoughts, Ben crept back in. If she had all this time ahead of her—maybe she could try to call him. Tonight could be dangerous, and if something did happen to her, she didn't want him to think that she didn't care about him.

So, as traffic got moving again, she used her free hand to dial him. It rang and rang, but he never picked up. It went to voicemail, and his achingly familiar voice reached her ears.

"This is Benjamin Chambers. Please leave a message after the tone."

Taylor took a deep breath, suddenly emotional at the sound of his voice. Eyes burning, she said, "Hi, Ben, it's me… I'm working the case still, as I'm sure you know. I, um, just wanted to let you know that I love you, and I hope you're okay. I'll be home tomorrow. I'm going to wrap this up tonight, I promise."

Silence dragged on as Taylor tried to think of what else to say. But by the time she'd come up with something, it was too late, and the time limit on the message had been reached. The call automatically ended.

But out loud, to herself, Taylor said, *"Wait for me."*

***

With her headlights turned off, Taylor crept into the empty parking lot in Dupont Circle. She put the car in park. There were no other vehicles in the lot—not even Calvin's. He should have been here at least twenty minutes before her. A twinge of worry hit her.

Where are you, Scott? Ducked low in the driver's seat, she scanned around for him, thinking maybe he'd hidden somewhere. But nothing but an empty lot surrounded her, and across the road was Four Acres Park. No dog walkers milled around; no drunk teenagers wandered the night. It was after midnight on a Tuesday, and the yellow glow from the streetlights illuminated the deserted area. Other than that, it was a ghost town.

Taylor had no other option but to call Calvin again. But this time, when she pressed the phone to her ear, it went straight to voicemail. Her stomach dropped. Suspicious, Taylor peered around again. Belasco's warning came back. The betrayal. Was this it? That would be extremely poor timing.

Memories flashed through Taylor's mind. All the time she'd spent with Calvin Scott. In her heart, she felt like she could trust him—she always had. But it was her mind that told her otherwise. And Taylor knew that sometimes, the mind was right, and the heart was wrong. Whatever the betrayal was, she needed to be prepared for it.

But now wasn't the time. A woman's life was in danger. Taylor hadn't even called Winchester yet; she'd gone totally rogue on this one, which she knew the higher ups wouldn't like of both her and Calvin. But if they got results—like they did last time—then she was sure she'd be forgiven. Or maybe she'd have to hand in her badge. Honestly, at this point, Taylor didn't care—she just wanted to stop Gabe and save Harriet from losing her life the same way the others did.

For now, she needed backup. *Close* backup. So she dug up a relic from inside her glove compartment—a police radio that she still kept charged and active, just in case she ever needed it. It wasn't necessarily common for FBI agents to bother carrying one, as usually they could use their phones for everything. But Taylor always had an inkling it may come in handy someday. Now was that time.

Turning on the radio, Taylor was able to access D.C.'s local patrol cops directly. Everything she said would reach whoever was available and in the area. Exactly what she needed. The radio crackled as she spoke into it:

"This is Special Agent Taylor Sage of the FBI, requesting immediate backup at Four Acres Park, Dupont Circle—we have a potential 187 in progress. All officers must execute discretion while approaching the scene. Suspect is Gabe French, nineteen, a Caucasian male, wanted in connection with three other homicides. Suspect may be seen wearing dark clothing and walking with a young woman, who I suspect is his next victim."

She prayed that would catch someone's attention fast, because she didn't have time to waste making phone calls. As for right now, there was no sign of her partner anywhere. Going solo was a risk Taylor would have to take.

With that, Taylor left her car, into the night. A cold breeze cut through her blazer, raising the goosebumps on her arms. She found herself standing alone in the parking lot, listening for something—anything—to make a sound. But D.C. was eerily quiet.

Sucking in a breath, Taylor dashed across the street. Once at the fence that lined the park, she crept along until she found the entrance, the same spot she'd been just days ago when she fought against George Fields in chess. Compared to then, it was a ghost town: completely empty, save for the trees, the benches, the garbage cans. It wasn't a very large park, and a snake-like path wound through it.

There wasn't a soul in sight. No Calvin. And certainly no killer. But Taylor was right about this one—she had to be. She'd seen it on French's computer. He was going to be here. It was just a matter of *when.*

Right?

Doubt swirled through her as she entered the park, keeping her back low. She felt for the familiar shape of her gun in its holster under her blazer as she crept along the wall. It was her safety net. But no matter how deep she got into the park, she saw no one. No bodies, either. Which could very well mean that Harriet Fleming was still alive.

Taylor's heart began to pound so loud in her ears that she could no longer listen to the sounds of the park. Maybe this was a mistake. Maybe she'd fucked up again, and she was chasing her tail like a fool. Maybe those officers would arrive and know she'd wasted their time too.

And what the hell was she thinking coming here so quickly, anyway? And without calling Quantico, no less. She had been so blinded by the idea of saving Harriet that she didn't even think to try to find Harriet's contact information and call her herself. Maybe the girl was still okay; maybe Gabe hadn't grabbed her yet.

All of these insecure thoughts swarmed Taylor's mind, and she wanted nothing more than to silence them. When had she grown so doubtful of herself? So distrusting of those around her?

In terms of her emotionality and decision-making, this had probably been Taylor's messiest case ever. Sure, she had made progress in the end—but the path to get here was riddled with emotion, with doubt, insecurity. It wasn't like her. She'd always been a bad sleeper, but the nightmares and insomnia seemed to increase tenfold over the past week. There was no denying it: her home situation with Ben had bled into her work, and it was affecting her decision-making. A sense of shame hung over her. This wasn't what a good agent was meant to be like.

Though, what she felt the most guilt for was her doubt of Calvin, even though he still wasn't here. Maybe the betrayal was not showing up on time or getting lost along the way. Would he really leave her out here to potential danger without a reason? Could it be negligence? She didn't know; all she knew was that he still wasn't here, he still hadn't called her. Maybe he decided to report her insolent behavior to the higher-ups. For that, she wouldn't blame him. Taylor had gone completely off the books in the name of the greater good. Her reasons were sound. But her methods weren't how the FBI did things.

Still, if she could save Harriet's life—all of this would be worth it. Every sleepless night, every piece of paranoia, and every bit of flack she'd get from Winchester. All worth it.

Suddenly—a twig snapped. Taylor jolted back to the present.

Her heart jumped. She sucked in a breath and took in the dark park. The clouds above parted, giving way to the moon's light, bathing the park in a silvery hue… but still, she saw nothing.

The sound had come from behind a tree on the other side of the park. In order for Taylor to get there, she had to expose herself and walk across. Either that, or go all the way around…

She didn't know what to do. But she kept listening, tuning her ears to even the smallest sound.

And that was when she heard it—a mumble. It was garbled, but distinctively human. Taylor didn't think—she just moved. Walking briskly with her back bent low, she darted toward the tree, where she swore she'd heard the sound. *Almost there. Just a little farther.*

She kept moving. Faster and faster.

I'll save you. I promise.

Then, right before the tree, Taylor felt a sudden warmth behind her.

Somebody was behind her. Every hair on her neck stood on end. On instinct, she went to grab her gun. To spin around and shoot whoever they were.

But the cool metal of a knife pressed against her throat.

A low, crackly voice whispered in her ear, breath hot against her neck: "Don't you move a muscle."

CHAPTER TWENTY SEVEN

"You scream and you die," he said.

Every fiber in Taylor's body turned to stone. His hot, sour breath reached her nose, and her stomach curled with disgust. Was this how she'd die? In the middle of a park in a city that meant nothing to her, her throat slit by a mere *child?*

Swallowing, Taylor felt the knife tremble against her throat. He was shaking. Maybe it was nerves, or maybe excitement. Either way, Taylor wouldn't dare move—it was too dangerous. She knew what this man was capable of. This very knife that was held up to her was most likely the same knife that had already stolen three—potentially four—lives.

But maybe, if she spoke, she could get something out of him.

"W-who are you?" she stammered innocently. She could convince him she was just an innocent bystander. A nobody. Buy enough time for the other officers to arrive, or for Calvin to finally show up. Maybe he wouldn't kill her. Maybe she'd get to live another day, to see Ben again, to fix her marriage. To adopt a child. Start the life she'd always truly wanted.

All of these sentimental thoughts began running a train through her mind as the knife remained on her throat, only millimetres away from ending it all. She'd always thought getting her throat slit would be a terrible way to die. Quick, but not quick enough. Surely, she'd feel enough of the blood drain out first. Be aware of every second her lifeforce faded away.

Oddly, faces of the many victims she'd seen throughout the years flashed through her mind too. They say some people can never forget a face—well, Taylor could never forget the faces of the dead, no matter how many she'd seen. She remembered one case when she was still a grunt cop when she'd answered a distress call from a woman, only to find out that she was too late—by the time she'd arrived at the girl's apartment, her boyfriend had slit her throat, left her there to bleed dry on the white carpet. Taylor still remembered the outfit the girl wore—pajamas—and the frozen expression on her face.

So many cases like that flashed in her memory. Was she about to become another one? Another dead face to live in another cop's memory? She didn't want it to end like this. But this was one situation she currently had no control over.

At least not yet.

Taylor held onto hope. She'd find a way out of this. She just needed time.

"Please," she stammered again.

"Don't act innocent with me," Gabe whispered, then his free hand jabbed the gun on her belt, hidden beneath her blazer. "I know you're a cop. You *smell* like one. Filthy animal."

Damn it. Taylor's teeth clenched. But she wasn't about to give in and accept it. There had to be a way. Her thoughts raced to find something else, but Gabe beat her to it.

"Just walk, and don't reach for that gun," he said. The pressure from the knife lifted, only slightly, and Taylor's thundering heart momentarily calmed. Gabe continued to hover the blade over her throat as he directed her toward the tree, which was next to a cast iron bench.

As they drew closer, Taylor held her breath to keep the knife as far away from her as she could. Then, she made out a shape at the base of the tree. She squinted harder to see, momentarily forgetting the situation she was in with her *own* death in Gabe French's hands.

A young woman was slumped against the base of the tree, her head hanging low. Her mouth was gagged by a cloth. With bedraggled brown hair tied back in a bun and a white uniform still on, Taylor recognized her as Harriet Fleming—"The Queen of U-Street."

Panic surged through her. She was too late. All this time, all this effort spent… and she couldn't even save the victim in the end.

And now, maybe Taylor was going to die for it too. Defeat slammed hard on her shoulders. In that moment, Taylor felt like nothing in her life had ever mattered at all.

But then—movement. Harriet's leg twitched. And Taylor's resolve burst back to life. Harriet wasn't dead at all—just unconscious.

I'm not too late.

Gabe pulled Taylor's gun from her belt and said, "You won't be needing this."

As soon as the gun was gone, he kicked her harshly in the back. The force sent ripples of pain through her. Taylor landed next to the cast iron bench. Gabe tossed the gun aside, into the grass—Taylor could dive for it, but it was a few strides away, and he still had that butcher knife pointed right at her.

But now that Taylor was facing him, she had a moment to take in his appearance.

A tall, lanky boy, who still held the posture of an awkward teenager, glared down at her. In the moonlight, Taylor could make out the crater-like scars on his face, and the deep scowl that made him look like an old man with the body of a teen. He wore a black hoodie with the hood up, concealing messy red hair. Taylor had never seen so much anger, so much hate, on somebody so young.

This had to be about more than chess. He was clearly sick, disturbed. But there was no excuse for what Gabe had done. He had to be stopped. Taylor couldn't give up yet. She needed to buy time—officers should have been arriving any second.

And where the hell is Scott?

Taylor tensed as Gabe stormed up to her. Fear took hold as he descended upon her—but all he did was dig into her pocket and take her cuffs. He slapped one on her wrist with the other end to the cast iron bench. Taylor tried to tug her arm away, but the weight of the bench was tremendous—she lay there like a helpless doll. No weapon. No strength to move.

"There, that should keep you put," Gabe said. His features relaxed, and a hint of a smile tugged at his lips. "You know, I've never had a witness before. You're lucky. You get to see what real strategy is before you die."

Stall him. Keep everyone alive. These were the only words that flew through Taylor's head as she mustered up the words, "Gabe, you don't have to do this."

His eyebrow twitched. "You know my name."

"I do. Of course." She could tell Gabe had an ego—stoking it might keep him busy for long enough. "I've seen your chess matches. On YouTube. They're incredible."

Squinting, he stepped closer to Taylor. She tried not to cower away, to show fear. But that butcher knife still had the moonlight trapped in it, gleaming in Gabe's right hand as though hungry to stab something.

"They were, weren't they?" Gabe mused. The knife relaxed, and his eyes glanced up at the stars for a moment before landing on her. The crazed look in them sent a chill up Taylor's spine. "Those days are over, though, aren't they? You know, I was suspended from participating in tournaments for a while. All my life, chess was the one thing I had. The only thing that stood out about me. And they took it away from me."

This time, he took a step back, closer to Harriet, who was still knocked out. Taylor began to sweat. No—she'd rather him be closer to her than to Harriet. Gabe had made it clear that his intention was to make Taylor watch him kill her. She couldn't let that happen.

"They shouldn't have done that," Taylor said. "You were a great chess player. The best."

Gabe halted. She breathed out in relief. It was working.

"You should have won that tournament," Taylor said. "Not Artemy Volkov."

"Oh?" Gabe's interest was piqued. "You know a lot. Maybe you aren't such a filthy pig after all." He sighed longingly. "You're right, though; they shouldn't have taken it away from me. But you know, I should thank them, and Volkov too. I had so much time alone in my apartment. So much time to think, and no one to play against… I tried playing online, I did, but it just wasn't satisfying enough. I needed to get my hands on some pieces."

His eyes flashed. That smile curled at his lips again.

"But not long ago, it hit me. Playing chess the traditional way—it's not enough, either. It's juvenile. It's the old way. But me—I could come up with a better way. A real way. With real stakes, a game truly worth playing."

Taylor recoiled with disgust at his words. It really was all just a game to him. She thought of Margot Withers, Liam Stoll, and Michael West—real people with lives, families, hopes, dreams… all snubbed out because of one sick person's twisted game.

She couldn't let him win this one.

"And if you're wondering why I'm doing this," Gabe continued, admiring his knife, "then, well, just imagine what it was like to be that one bullied kid with the twisted mind. You know the one. No parents. No one to raise him. I had teachers who helped me, sure, but even still… they wouldn't adopt me. I even asked one if they would. Someone I truly trusted. But even she rejected me. My heart broke. I never had a family."

Clearly, the foster care system had failed him. And Taylor did empathize with that. She could only imagine how hard it must have been to grow up alone and never get adopted. To always feel unwanted and alone, like there was something inherently wrong with him. But this type of evil couldn't be helped, no matter what.

"But I did have chess," Gabe continued. "It's just too bad—I was truly hoping to attract the attention of someone who could play the game back. But none of you figured out how."

"How?" Taylor instinctively tried to stand, to rush at him, but the cuff on her wrist pulled her back down to the earth. She was desperate to know, to understand if there was anything she could have done sooner to prevent all of this.

Gabe just snickered. "How, indeed."

In one quick motion, Gabe rushed at Harriet and lifted her up by her wrist. Taylor barely had time to scream, to tell him no, before the knife lifted in the air. It was too late—he was going to stab her, and Taylor was powerless to stop it.

But suddenly, a voice: "Drop the weapon and put your hands up!"

Gabe froze, still holding Harriet up. But the knife was in the air, away from her.

Taylor dared to glance away, just in time to see Calvin limping up with his gun out, pointed right at Gabe. A fresh gash ran down the side of his face, causing blood to leak down his pale skin. He looked like he'd just walked out of a car crash.

"I said drop the weapon!" Calvin repeated, his voice deeper, angrier than Taylor had ever heard.

Gabe's entire demeanor changed. He still held the knife up, but his eyes filled with fear, and all the cockiness, the delusions of grandeur washed away. He looked like a terrified child again.

"Okay," he stammered. "Okay, don't shoot."

"Drop the *fucking* weapon!"

Gabe's knees trembled like they were about to buckle. He went to move. Taylor expected to see him drop the knife. He was clearly ready to resign.

But a resounding gunshot fired off.

Taylor's ears rang with pain. Tinnitus took over, and everything around her slowed. She couldn't hear. Couldn't think. Her head pounded as she lifted her eyes to the scene in front of her. D.C. police officers had emerged and were surrounding them.

Harriet had woken up. Officers surrounded her as her eyes bulged, looking at what was in front of her in complete shock.

And when Taylor took it in too, bile rose to her throat.

Gabe French lay lifeless in the grass, blood pooling from the wound in his chest.

CHAPTER TWENTY EIGHT

Standing outside of the interrogation room, Taylor bit on her knuckle as she watched through the double-sided glass. Inside, Calvin was being questioned by Special Agent Brady and a slew of other higher-ups, while Winchester was at Taylor's side. They'd both been deemed too close to him to make a proper assessment of his crime; hence Brady and the others were called in to deal with it.

Taylor's eyes burned as she watched. Calvin looked exhausted as he slumped in the chair, while Brady across from him was talking, making dramatic hand gestures as he did. They couldn't hear what was going on; they were told not to listen. But it didn't look good.

Agent Calvin Scott had acted rashly, everyone had said. Gabe French was going to drop the knife. He'd transformed from a violent killer to a scared kid in front of Taylor's eyes, and while she didn't pity him… she knew damn well that shooting a perp while he may have been surrendering wasn't a good look for the bureau.

And there were a lot of witnesses.

Most of the D.C. officers who had responded to Taylor's distress call had arrived with Calvin and had been there front and center to see exactly what Taylor had seen. She knew it wasn't good.

But she also knew Calvin Scott.

The first thing he'd said after Gabe had collapsed was: "Shit—I didn't mean to." He'd said he was going for Gabe's shoulder, on the arm still holding the knife, but his aim was off. It was a huge mistake to make, especially for someone with as much training and skill as Calvin was meant to have.

Emotion took over her, and she did everything to keep in her tears. Winchester was still right beside her, his breathing labored as he watched the scene.

Through all of this, Taylor had realized something.

Belasco's warning had never been about Calvin betraying Taylor herself—it had been about him betraying the law. Betraying himself, and his own values, in a desperate attempt to save her, and to save the victim. Taylor knew Calvin would never recklessly shoot somebody—let alone in the chest—in his right mind. On top of that, he had gotten into a car accident on the way over but had *still* made it there to help her.

"He doesn't deserve this," Taylor choked out.

Winchester looked at her and sighed. "You were there, Sage. You know what you saw. Scott shot the guy through the heart."

Taylor's chest tightened, torn between loyalty to her partner and an obligation to tell the truth. "He didn't mean to. It isn't that simple."

"Well, Brady and everyone in there are trying to get into Scott's mind and figure out why he acted so rashly. We don't care how young the guy is. We expect more of a federal agent. Deaths can happen, but this one was preventable. Gabe French should be rotting in a prison cell, not a body bag."

"I know, Chief." Taylor looked back through the window, where Calvin had bags as deep as craters on his face. Special Agent Brady stood up and gave Calvin a nod before he left the interrogation room and left the other agents to talk to Calvin. He reconvened with Taylor and Winchester outside.

Taylor rushed at him. Special Agent Brady was a Quantico veteran; in his late fifties, he had silver hair and gray eyes. A guilty look laced them as he met Taylor's eager stare.

"What will happen to him?" was her first question.

"Well," Brady said, glancing between Taylor and Winchester, "the good news is, Gabe French was a serial killer, and it could be very reasonably argued that Agent Scott acted rashly to save Harriet Fleming's life. If Scott means what he says, then he was aiming for the shoulder. At best, that makes him a dangerously bad shot."

Taylor didn't like the sound of that.

Brandy continued, "But of the multiple eyewitnesses—you included, Special Agent Sage—not one of them has said what Agent Scott did was necessarily the right move."

"What's he got to say for himself?" Winchester asked.

"He admitted that he acted rashly," Brady replied. "He said that he was desperate and disoriented from his car crash. But car crash or not, he's trained to know when not to shoot. He shouldn't have had his gun out if he was disoriented."

What Taylor really wanted to know was what came next. "What will happen to him?" she asked again.

"Well, he can't stay in Quantico, that's for sure," Brady said. "We're thinking an immediate transfer would be good, and a month of unpaid leave. Maybe some mandated therapy. If he's lucky, Gabe

French won't have anyone hoping to bring Scott to trial over the death. Based on the kid's history, though, I don't foresee that happening."

Taylor's stomach dropped. She knew Gabe French had no one. But if Calvin was transferred out of Quantico, that would mean he wouldn't be her partner anymore. He'd be gone, and she'd be assigned someone new.

But Taylor didn't want someone new. After everything, she was finally realizing how much she could trust Calvin Scott, on a personal level. And yes, he had made a mistake—but personal trust was hard to build. It had taken her and her old partner in Oregon, Jenkins, a long time to warm up to each other. But Taylor had clicked with Calvin fast, faster than she'd expected. He was compassionate and kind, with a strong moral compass—but he wasn't afraid to be fierce, either. Taylor loved these traits in him.

And now he was going away. She glanced back into the glass, where he was rubbing his hands over his eyes. Choked up, Taylor couldn't speak. She didn't want this for him; he deserved better.

Brady continued, "Agent Scott has blood on his hands. I'm not saying Gabe French didn't deserve to die—he did. But that's not how we do things."

"Unfortunately, I agree," Winchester said. "Agent Scott will be thirty soon. He's not that young. We can't give him a free pass. This was a huge oversight. We're just lucky the guy he killed was a piece of shit holding a knife at an innocent woman. Otherwise, things would be looking a lot worse for him."

Taylor's mind raced. Of course it could be worse, but was there nothing she could do to save him from this fate?

"I know he made a mistake," she blabbered, desperate to help, "but as his partner, I have to say—Agent Scott has been rock solid. He has always been there when I've needed him. And come on, we have to cut him some slack; he got in a damn car accident before, and—" Realizing her anger was coming out, Taylor paused and took a breath. "He's a good agent," she finally said. "I couldn't ask for a better partner. If you leave him with me, I promise I'll talk to him about how this can never happen again."

The two men exchanged an uncomfortable look. Taylor knew her attempts were fruitless, but she had to try. She'd never forgive herself if she didn't.

"I'm sorry, Sage." Winchester patted her on the shoulder. "Agent Scott will be okay. But we can't have him here anymore, at least not now. I'll be taking Special Agent Brady's advice and calling for Scott's immediate termination from Quantico."

No. It couldn't end like this. There had to be another way. But Taylor had nothing. Once more, that sense of powerlessness overtook her. She had been powerless to save some of the victims. Powerless to save Angie all those years ago. And now, powerless to help another person she cared about.

"It's a hell of a lot better than prison," Brady added, looking at Taylor as she tried to come up with another excuse.

"And we can't just walk around shooting criminals, Sage," Winchester said. "You know that." Suddenly, his face hardened. "And let's not forget here that you were acting way out of turn too, Sage. I commend you for catching Gabe French and saving Harriet Fleming. But you went way off the books."

She looked at her feet. "I know, Chief. I'm sorry."

His large hand was suddenly on her shoulder. He squeezed reassuringly. "You're a good agent, Sage. Damn good. But you're obsessive, and Scott isn't the only one with impulse control issues." He paused. This was getting too personal, and Taylor wished Brady wasn't there listening. "I'd like you to take a week off again and sort yourself out," he said.

Panic instantly struck her. She didn't want to spend a week off, facing nothing but her own demons. "Chief, I—"

"It's an order, Sage," Winchester said. "No buts." She opened her mouth to object, but he patted her once on the back. "Go finish up your statements, then go home to your husband, Taylor. We aren't the only ones who need you."

Taylor knew they weren't going to let her back down or let her talk to Calvin while he was still at HQ.

So, she left for now—but she had every intention of seeing him again before he left Quantico.

***

Taylor pulled her car to a stop outside of a bungalow on a dark and quiet street, in a small town only thirty minutes away from the Quantico headquarters. Taylor had had a general idea of where Calvin lived, but she didn't realize it was so close. No wonder he had always been so punctual.

His car was parked in the driveway, and despite it being nearly four in the morning, the lights inside were on behind the curtains. He had been sent home only an hour before, while Taylor had stuck around a bit longer to hash out the details and make her final case about Calvin staying. It was all to no avail; they'd made it clear Calvin was suspended immediately and was being sent across the country. They didn't tell her where. He'd left the building before Taylor had a chance to talk to him.

So, she came here.

Nervousness swam through her mind. Maybe it was inappropriate—but she knew he'd be leaving town soon, and she had a long drive ahead of her to get home. She needed to talk to Calvin first.

She got out of the car, into the cold night. September was just around the corner. Taylor didn't imagine she'd be going into the fall with a new partner. She'd expected her and Calvin to work together for years, to grow as a team. Especially being so close in age, she never thought he would go anywhere unless either of them moved.

As she approached his door, her nerves continued to rise. She took slow, careful breaths, and put one foot after the other until she reached it. A beat, and she knocked. For a few moments, nothing happened—but then something clicked behind the door, and Calvin opened it, still wearing his clothes from earlier. He looked like he'd been hit by a bus, but before he was interrogated for the shooting, he'd been sent to a doctor for a quick checkup. Nothing was badly injured in the crash, so she'd been told. His head had just been a bit banged up.

"Taylor?" he said, brows raised. "What are you doing here?"

"Scott, I—" She lowered her head in shame, unable to hold his gaze. "I tried to vouch for you. I really did. There was nothing I could do."

"Hey." He relaxed against the doorframe, and a half-smile tugged at his lips. "Sage, you're not the one who fucked up. I did. I'm lucky I'm not going to jail."

"You did it to save an innocent person's life."

"But I didn't need to go that far." His jaw tightened as he looked down. "I killed someone, Sage. I've never done that before."

Taylor didn't know what to say. She'd never taken a life either. She'd shot people before, of course, but never fatally. And never right to the heart. As agents, they were taught that lethal force must only be used if absolutely necessary. Taylor was willing to do it, of course. Someday, she probably would.

"You hit him right in the heart," Taylor said. "What happened? Were you really aiming for his shoulder?"

"I was," Calvin admitted. "But I was seeing double. My head was killing me. I shouldn't have taken the shot. I'm lucky I hit Gabe and not Harriet."

That was true. Calvin should have known better. But Taylor couldn't bring herself to be frustrated with him; he was already being punished for what he'd done.

Calvin averted his eyes. "Taylor, I can't hide from this one. In that moment, the only thing I was thinking about was saving you and that woman. So, I just shot. It didn't hit me what I'd actually done until he was dead on the ground."

Hugging herself, Taylor looked away. "Where will you be sent?"

"Funny enough, Portland," he said.

Taylor almost laughed. She had worked as an agent in Portland for years but had traded that life for Virginia with Ben. So they could get away and start a family.

"They'll love you there," she said.

"Except I'm not going."

Taylor's heart jerked in her chest. "What?" she asked. His words gave her whiplash.

Calvin wore a sad smile. "While everyone was evaluating me, trying to decide how best to handle this… I handed in my badge, Taylor. I'm not an agent anymore."

"What? Why? I don't understand. You're a good agent, Scott." Her voice shook as she spoke. She didn't want to accept this was how things ended for him.

"I'm not." He shook his head. Although his eyes were full of sadness, he still smiled. "I fucked up big time. I'm gonna have to deal with it now."

"Then why are you packing? Where are you going?"

"My mother's, back in New York," he said. "I'm gonna take some time off before I figure out what I should do with my life."

As much as it hurt her, she had nothing left to ask him. Whatever Calvin chose to do next was his choice, and his choice alone. But she wanted him to know that, despite what had happened, he was still a fine agent—someone she would trust her life with. She regretted that during their last case together, Taylor had doubted him because of a misinterpreted warning from a fortune teller. Thankfully, Calvin never needed to know that.

“You were a good agent, Scott,” she said. “Having you as my partner was an honor.”

“Thanks, Sage. Likewise.”

Taylor took a moment to glance into his house behind him. A black and white spotted cat was perched on top of a couch, and behind a wall, she could catch a glimpse of his tidy living room and massive TV. On the wall next to the door was a photo of him and an older woman—his mother. And it hit Taylor how little she got to know about Calvin’s personal life. It hurt that she’d never get to learn.

Earlier on the case, when he’d given her some breadcrumbs of his past in school, she had felt like he was finally opening up to her. Maybe she was being dramatic about all of this—it wasn’t like Calvin was dead or going to jail. He would be okay, but still, she could already feel the impact his loss would have on her life.

Time was ticking on, and awkwardness filled the air as they both ran out of words to say. But at the very least, Taylor wanted to end this on good terms. She extended her hand. Calvin met her eyes once before he shook it firmly, then he rolled his eyes and laughed. Taylor yelped as he pulled her into a hug, and she found herself trapped in his arms.

“Thanks, Sage,” he said, patting her back. “I’ll miss you. I hope things work out with your husband. You deserve to be happy, okay?”

With her face pressed against his chest, Taylor wanted to cry. She hugged him back, daring to let her emotions bleed through. But she wouldn’t let him see her cry. Pulling away, she forced a smile to hide her sadness.

“Goodbye, Calvin,” she said, before she left him for the last time.

CHAPTER TWENTY NINE

As Taylor pulled into her driveway at home, the clock read six a.m. The sun was beginning to peek over the horizon, casting a silver hue on the roof of her home with Ben. She put the car in park but didn't get out—she just crammed her palms into her eyes as exhaustion weighed on her like a lead vest.

She'd cried the whole way here. Not only about losing Calvin as her partner, but about the state of everything in her life since she'd moved to Virginia. She thought about her life in Portland before—it hadn't been perfect. In fact, it had been stagnating, and Taylor had longed for more. But she never expected things would turn out like this.

Then again, if she hadn't moved here, she wouldn't have met Calvin at all. And she was grateful that she did. His optimism and tenacity wasn't something she'd ever forget, and he would always be one of her most cherished colleagues. She hoped that after the bureau's careful review, he would be reinstated as an agent, and they could work together again. Maybe someday. Nothing was impossible.

But losing Calvin had made her think, long and hard, about her life as she'd driven through the early morning to get here. Taylor had lost many things in her life. Her sister. Her baby. Her fertility. Her partner.

She couldn't bear to lose another person she cared about.

And so she had to make things right with Ben. Losing her husband on top of all of this would destroy her.

Their last dinner together had been a step in the right direction, and it seemed that Ben was really willing to try. Which meant that he didn't completely hate her for lying, and maybe, he could still see a future with her. Even if that meant no biological children. Taylor had to hold onto hope, even if it was small; it was all she had left.

He was definitely still sleeping—he'd never called her back after the voicemail she'd left. Taylor needed to catch a few hours herself. But Taylor planned on making dinner for Ben while he was at work and cleaning the whole house, so when he did get home, he would see that she was willing to try too. She thought about his favorite meals, and what she could make him to show him she cared.

With heavy limbs, Taylor dragged herself out of the car. The salty ocean air wafted into her nostrils, and she took a moment to glance up at the early-morning sky. She breathed in deep. Felt the coolness in her lungs.

Things were going to be okay. Even if she didn't have Calvin anymore, they had done their jobs. They had saved Harriet Fleming and had stopped Gabe French from ever killing again. In the end, Taylor was let off the hook for doing things her own way instead of checking with Winchester, only because her results had worked. If she hadn't been so reckless, then Harriet would be dead, and Gabe would be alive, hunting his next victim.

Ideally, the situation would have ended with no further casualties, but the trade-off was worth it.

As Taylor walked up to the house, she noticed the light was on inside through the window. That was odd—it wasn't like Ben to not turn off the lights when he went to bed. Frowning, Taylor dug her keys from her pocket and opened the door. Maybe he had fallen asleep on the couch, although that wasn't like him either.

But when the door opened, the first thing she saw was a suitcase by the stairs.

It was tightly shut, but clearly full. Taylor could barely even process the sight of it before Ben trotted down the stairs, two more suitcases in his hands.

He froze when he saw her, his brown eyes locked onto hers. She froze too. Unable to accept what she was seeing. Did he plan a trip without telling her? Was he going to visit his parents? If so—why didn't he call her? Didn't he get her voicemail?

All of these questions fired off in her mind, even though Taylor could see that this was far too many suitcases for a trip. This was something else. A sense of sheer panic took hold of her, and her heart began to thrum loudly in her ears. *No, no—this can't be happening.*

Ben reached the first floor, awkwardly tossing his suitcases next to the other one. He wrung his hand along the back of his neck as Taylor gawked at him, wide-eyed.

He was leaving her.

She could feel it throughout every fiber of her being before he even spoke.

"Taylor, I…," he trailed off, unable to hold her eyes. "I'm sorry."

"What's going on?" Her bottom lip trembled. Taylor couldn't keep it together anymore—when her eyes burned, the tears free fell without her permission. But she didn't care. All she cared about were the answers to this nightmarish scene playing out in front of her. All she cared about was waking up from this never-ending hell.

Ben sighed and threw his arms up. He looked exhausted, and broken blood vessels dotted around his eyes, like he'd been crying. "I'm sorry, Taylor. But I can't do this anymore."

"What?" Her voice came out weak, pathetic. "Where are you going? I don't understand," she said, even though she did understand. She just didn't want to believe it. "Did you get my voicemail?"

Guilt laced Ben's stare and his posture shrunk, but still, he said, "I just… can't do it. You know me, Taylor. You know I've always wanted kids. I was raised to want kids, to start a family—it's in my DNA."

A strong sense of betrayal and despair tore through her like a hurricane. She felt powerless, out of control, just like she had earlier when she couldn't save Calvin. Somehow, this was worse. It was like everything in Taylor's life was falling apart all at once, and the weight of those walls crashing down would pummel her to death. Ben was the last support beam. She needed him.

"Ben, no," she croaked. She wasn't one to beg—but in this moment, all she wanted was her husband's warm embrace, and he was *leaving* her? All because of something she had no control over?

"God, I'm sorry…," his body trembled. "I was hoping I'd be gone before you got home. This isn't easy, Taylor. I do love you, but I'm confused. I want to start a family."

"So do I," she pleaded. "We could adopt, we could—"

"Hon, stop," Ben cut her off. "I'm sorry. I just… I need to go stay with my sister for a while. I need time to think. The truth is, I have to figure out if our life together is worth never having kids. Never having my own family."

"There are many ways to have a family," she said. "We can still have one. It doesn't have to be traditional."

She thought of Gabe French, how sick and twisted he had been, how the foster care system had failed him. There were so many kids out there who needed to be loved, to be cared for. Taylor knew that together, she and Ben could provide a child a wonderful life. Sure, her job was risky—but she would give it everything she had.

"We could adopt," Taylor said. "We could give a child an amazing life. Even two children. You would still be their father, Ben. Or we could look into a surrogate. So many couples do that. I wouldn't mind, really. It doesn't have to end this way."

"I don't want someone else's child," he said bitterly, "and I don't want the child of a woman I don't love."

She couldn't believe his coldness. It bled through her feeling of sadness, making her bitter. Over this past while, she felt like she didn't even know the man that she married. He had become callous beneath a veil of niceties, and she wondered if maybe this had always been in him, and she just hadn't seen it.

But memories flashed through her mind. Happier memories. Their wedding day, moving in together, all of the drunk conversations they'd had about how much they loved each other and couldn't wait to be together forever. How could Taylor let all of it go so easily? More importantly, how could Ben?

Did their time together mean nothing to him?

She thought of their wedding. It had been such a white day, so pure, full of naïve happiness and optimism. Her father had walked her down the aisle. Her mother had never been prouder. And Taylor had imagined that Angie was there with them, and that she loved Ben as much as the rest of her family did.

Ben's wedding vows entered her memory and made her stomach sick. She remembered feeling like everything in her world was right, for the first time ever, as he'd said, *"Taylor Sage, you're the most courageous, outstanding, strongest woman I've ever met. I've never known anyone so selfless. You're a little reckless sometimes, and you scare the shit out of me—but that's why I fell for you. You'll make an amazing wife, and an amazing mother to our children someday."*

Taylor wanted to throw up. Their entire relationship had been built on the promise of a family someday. It had always been a condition of being with Ben.

Could she really blame him for leaving her now?

"I'm sorry," he said again, grabbing his suitcases as he headed past her to the door. He opened it, letting in the early morning air, and tossed the first suitcase out, then the other. "I need time, okay?" he said, meeting her eyes.

But Taylor knew what "time" meant. He wasn't coming back. Ben Chambers had always wanted children, and Taylor couldn't give that to him. He would choose his dream over her, because *she* wasn't his dream. Even if he had been hers.

She said nothing, shocked and dumbfounded as Ben took his final suitcase and closed the door behind him. Taylor stared blankly at the door until she heard the sound of his car starting up. Snapping back to reality, she ran to the window and peered out, praying he'd turn back and change his mind.

But he didn't.

His car drove away and disappeared down the street, leaving Taylor shattered, broken, and alone.

***

Taylor wasn't sure how long she stood by that window where she had watched Ben leave—it could have been minutes, maybe an hour. But by the time she'd snapped out of her trance, the sun had fully risen, and she realized how alone she truly was.

She turned to face her living room, the bookshelves still stocked full of Ben's junk. They had bought this house with the intention of building a family around it. It was far too big for two people—and certainly far too big for Taylor by herself.

Back in Portland, before she'd moved in with Ben, she'd had her own apartment. Suddenly, she longed to go back to that spot in her past—back when things were simple. She missed that small apartment; it felt more like home to her than this place ever had.

Here she was in his giant house, completely alone. Sure, there were pictures of her and Ben on the walls. She even still had some furniture from when she'd had that old apartment. But this wasn't where she belonged.

She realized then that she hated it here.

Anger clawed its way through the despair. This wasn't her home. This was of Ben's choosing. How could he walk away and leave her like this? What kind of husband was he? Furious, Taylor tore up the stairs and into their room, where all of Ben's things had been removed from their bedroom. Of course, he had left all of his junk in the living room, but the bedroom had been emptied of all traces of her husband. No cologne by the vanity. He hadn't even bothered to close the drawer, which was left wide open and devoid of all Ben's clothing.

She looked down at her finger, at the ring he had put there with a promise of forever.

It was all a load of shit.

But despite it all, Taylor couldn't bring it in herself to hate Ben. The anger dissolved, and once again, the pain took over. Of course she didn't hate him—she loved him. She *wanted* to give him the life he wanted. If she could, she would do it in a heartbeat. Forget all those doubts she had before she knew about her infertility; if she could change one thing, it would be this. She would save her marriage.

Tears burned her eyes as she dove at the bed. It didn't even smell like him anymore; he'd been sleeping in the guest room, even when she wasn't home. It all killed her inside. Things weren't supposed to end this way. This wasn't how she saw her life ending up.

But this was what had happened. She curled up into the bed, finding some small solace in the comforter. She couldn't hide from this pain, not this time. There was no case to work. No crime to bury herself in so she could hide from her problems. No, this time, she allowed all her feelings in through a floodgate. Allowed herself to feel the pain in every muscle, every bone. With it, she sobbed miserably into her pillow.

And somewhere along the way, she drifted asleep, knowing that her life would never be the same again.

EPILOGUE

If someone had told Taylor only two months ago that she would be seeking comfort from a fortune teller over the departure of her husband, she would have laughed in their face. Told them it was the most ludicrous thing she'd ever heard. If there was one thing Taylor Sage had always been known for, it was her practicality. But these visits to the tarot reader had become her little secret.

And that was exactly where Taylor was now, staring down the door of Miriam Belasco's shop yet again.

She didn't know who else to turn to.

After Ben left earlier that day, Taylor had spent hours in bed, stuck in an endless cycle of crying and half falling asleep, only to be rocked awake by a nightmare. Now, the late-afternoon sun shone down on her, but the breeze from the ocean was cold. Taylor hugged herself, shivering. She knew her face was puffy and red, and that there would be no way to hide her pain from Belasco this time.

But in truth, she didn't care anymore.

She wanted answers more than she valued her pride at this moment. The unthinkable had happened: her husband had left her. If there was any hope of reclaiming the life they'd once had—the life they'd once wished for—then Taylor needed to know what to do next. She could argue that seeing Belasco had never brought her life anything more than anxiety, but she also knew that she had helped tremendously on actual cases. And so, at this point, Taylor was willing to give the woman some credibility. But perhaps, she needed to not take her words so literally.

So, she sucked in a breath and entered the store. It was strange, how she'd used to think of this place as so fake, so hokey, but the dark aura and smell of incense now comforted her. Belasco walked out from behind the curtain, looking as elusive and mysterious as ever. But when she saw the look on Taylor's face, a different expression took over the fortune teller.

No longer the wise and mysterious woman Taylor had become accustomed to, Belasco instead took on the appearance of a friend. Someone with true compassion on their face. Clearly, she could tell something horrible had happened. She didn't say a word—just wasted no time opening the curtain to allow Taylor to pass.

With her head down, Taylor followed Belasco into the back. The two women found themselves face to face, and Belasco delicately placed a hand on Taylor's shoulder and squeezed. Breathless, Taylor wanted to cry again—she didn't expect the simple touch of another person to have her so emotional. She hadn't even called her parents yet. She didn't have it in her to admit her shame; that her own lies, deceit, and neglect had led to her failed marriage. Her parents loved Ben. She did too.

"I'm glad you came," Belasco said, lifting her touch. "I'm happy to have you here."

Taylor simply nodded, too choked up to say much more than, "Thank you."

"Would you like to do a reading?" Belasco offered, floating over to the desk, where the tarot cards waited.

Taylor gave her answer by sitting down in her usual chair. Belasco sat down as well, peering at her with those dark eyes. A moment of silence passed as Belasco shuffled the cards, then arranged them into three decks.

"Do you have a specific question, Mrs. Sage?" Belasco asked, her voice delicate.

Hugging herself, Taylor sank in the chair. "Um…," she sniffled and looked away. This was humiliating. In truth, her rational mind knew that she needed a therapist more than a fortune teller. Yet still, Belasco was a virtual stranger, and Taylor would prefer to talk to her about her problems than anyone else. Maybe she wasn't such a stranger, after all.

"It happened," Taylor confessed. "What you predicted before, about somebody important leaving me."

"Ah." Belasco clasped her hands on the table. "I take it your husband is not with you today for a reason."

Head low, Taylor nodded. "Yes. He left me. I don't think he's coming back."

"I'm so sorry." Belasco offered Taylor a compassionate smile, the corners of her eyes crinkling. "Are you hoping the cards can shed light on the situation?"

"I guess I am," Taylor admitted. "I just… don't know where to go from here." She sucked in a breath. What she was about to say were three words she hadn't uttered many times in her life. Her pride often didn't allow it. But after everything that had happened, she had to say it: "I need help."

Belasco didn't look upon her with judgement—only kindness and understanding. "The cards can help you," Belasco assured. "Whether it's to help you understand your situation or shed some light on your future… they can help."

"I hope so," Taylor mumbled, because being here, doing this, was taking everything out of her. She had never felt so lost before.

"Let's get started then." Belasco's hand reached for the first pile of cards. A beat, and she flipped it up, revealing a card with a wheel on it. "First, we have The Wheel of Fortune, upright. This signals change. The inevitable cycle of fate."

Taylor thought on it. Certainly, this situation with Ben was inevitable. Taylor had always felt like there was truth to fate, but she'd always thought of it more in the practical sense, rather than cosmic. Things happened the way they were supposed to. In that sense, maybe she was always supposed to get shot, and Ben was always supposed to leave her. Even back when they swore their wedding vows—things were always going to end this way.

Her heart lurched. She wished she could have a chance to turn back the clock, but life didn't work that way. However, a glimpse into her future might steer her in the right direction.

"Next," Belasco said, flipping up the second card to reveal a card with a sword and a snake on it, "we have the Ace of Swords, upright. This could signify clarity. A major breakthrough in your life. Does that mean anything to you?"

Not necessarily, Taylor thought. Unless it meant she would find clarity about Ben and accept what she had done.

Taylor just shrugged, so Belasco continued.

"And finally," she said, flipping up the final card, "we have The Four of Wands, upright. This could mean home and community, a cause for celebration."

That sounded optimistic, but Taylor didn't understand how to read these the way Belasco did. She asked, "So what do you think it all means? This reading doesn't seem bad, right?" A bit of hope jumped in her chest.

Belasco's thin, pencilled eyebrows pulled together. "Well, the message is a little cryptic. I've drawn a lot of reversed cards for you, but all three of these are upright. Very interesting." She paused as she considered the meaning. "If I had to guess… fate seems to me to suggest an inevitable conclusion to something that has long haunted you. That is supported by the next card, which could be a major breakthrough in your life. Finally, the home, community, the cause for celebration…" Belasco's eyes flicked to Taylor's. Taylor's heart pounded as she eagerly awaited her reply. "Mrs. Sage, if I had to guess, I would say the cards are saying something—or some*one*—from your past might be returning to you."

Taylor's mind sprinted over the possibilities. Could it be about Ben? She hoped it was. This was what she felt like was her first "positive" reading. Maybe things with Ben had a chance to work out.

But as fast as the thought came, it dissolved away. Ben was hardly someone from her "past"—he was still her present. It hadn't even been eight hours since he'd walked out her door. But who else could it be? Calvin? No, he wasn't her "past" either, not yet.

Another thought struck Taylor like a bolt of lightning.

There was someone from Taylor's past who she had always been haunted by. A case that never left her mind. And recently, she'd been dreaming of her over and over again.

Angie.

It was impossible. As much as Taylor had always hoped Angie was somehow still alive, the chances were almost zero. They'd found the shred of her clothing in the woods, the last trace of her that ever existed, and that was almost two decades ago. If Angie were alive, she'd be thirty-six by now, two years older than Taylor.

There was no way she would have been alive and well all this time and not have contacted her younger sister or their family.

Unless she was still in danger. Unless she was held hostage.

Still, these cards had to mean something. And with the dreams, too—Taylor couldn't deny that it was all pointing to Angie. Maybe she was a fool for hoping, for setting herself up to be heartbroken all over again…

But now, Taylor had a reason to believe Angie could still be out there.

She wouldn't rest until she found out the truth.

NOW AVAILABLE FOR PRE-ORDER!

DON'T RUN
(A Taylor Sage FBI Suspense Thriller—Book 3)

A new serial killer haunts the city, leaving his victims' bodies with an eerie signature: a single orchid. Brilliant FBI Special Agent and BAU specialist Taylor Sage, battling her own demons, tries to ignore the tarot reader's riddles. But when she has no choice but to explore them, she may just wish she hadn't.

"Molly Black has written a taut thriller that will keep you on the edge of your seat… I absolutely loved this book and can't wait to read the next book in the series!"
—Reader review for Girl One: Murder

DON'T RUN is book #3 of a brand-new series by critically acclaimed and #1 bestselling mystery and suspense author Molly Black.

With the FBI, police and local horticulturalists stumped, it's up to Taylor to connect the dots. But as Taylor's marriage crumbles around her and she struggles to connect with her new partner, she's under more pressure than ever to find this killer—before he finds her first.

Could the tarot reader's clue provide a spark of inspiration?

Or will this case be Taylor's last?

A complex psychological crime thriller full of twists and turns and packed with heart-pounding suspense, the TAYLOR SAGE mystery series will make you fall in love with a brilliant new female protagonist and keep you turning pages late into the night.

Future books in the series will be available soon.

Molly Black

Bestselling author Molly Black is author of the MAYA GRAY FBI suspense thriller series, comprising nine books (and counting); of the RYLIE WOLF FBI suspense thriller series, comprising six books (and counting); of the TAYLOR SAGE FBI suspense thriller series, comprising three books (and counting); and of the KATIE WINTER FBI suspense thriller series, comprising six books (and counting).

An avid reader and lifelong fan of the mystery and thriller genres, Molly loves to hear from you, so please feel free to visit www.mollyblackauthor.com to learn more and stay in touch.

BOOKS BY MOLLY BLACK

MAYA GRAY MYSTERY SERIES
GIRL ONE: MURDER (Book #1)
GIRL TWO: TAKEN (Book #2)
GIRL THREE: TRAPPED (Book #3)
GIRL FOUR: LURED (Book #4)
GIRL FIVE: BOUND (Book #5)
GIRL SIX: FORSAKEN (Book #6)
GIRL SEVEN: CRAVED (Book #7)
GIRL EIGHT: HUNTED (Book #8)
GIRL NINE: GONE (Book #9)

RYLIE WOLF FBI SUSPENSE THRILLER
FOUND YOU (Book #1)
CAUGHT YOU (Book #2)
SEE YOU (Book #3)
WANT YOU (Book #4)
TAKE YOU (Book #5)
DARE YOU (Book #6)

TAYLOR SAGE FBI SUSPENSE THRILLER
DON'T LOOK (Book #1)
DON'T BREATHE (Book #2)
DON'T RUN (Book #3)

KATIE WINTER FBI SUSPENSE THRILLER
SAVE ME (Book #1)
REACH ME (Book #2)
HIDE ME (Book #3)
BELIEVE ME (Book #4)
HELP ME (Book #5)
FORGET ME (Book #6)

Lightning Source UK Ltd.
Milton Keynes UK
UKHW010159070223
416581UK00003B/143